Abducted

Book 8

Marti Talbott's Highlander Series

By

Marti Talbott

-

© All Rights Reserved

Editor: *Frankie Sutton*

CHAPTER I

It was about this child Laird Justin MacGreagor worried most. She had his determination and her mother's defined features, but Paisley had something more than most women. Born second eldest, her long hair went from pale yellow to white by the time she reached the age of sixteen. Her hair made her blue eyes mesmerizing and warriors, young and old alike, could not seem to keep from gawking at her. The moment she entered the great hall, a laird's place of constant clan business, the men quieted just to watch her -- a habit Justin found extremely irritating. His daughter liked it even less and often glared at the men or crossed her eyes.

One day two MacDuff brothers mentioned her extraordinary beauty to another man in a marketplace, who told another and another. Word began to spread all across Scotland and Justin MacGreagor's nightmare had only just begun.

*

For the most part, life in the MacGreagor clan was pleasant. The forests surrounding their glen offered sufficient hunting and the river behind the village held an abundance of fish. Flocks of sheep supplied mutton for food and wool for their clothing, cows gave them milk and farmers raised vegetables in the adjoining valley. Always there were birds chirping in the trees and the sweet smell of Scots Pine in the forest filled the air when the breeze blew just right.

Old and new cottages bordered meandering paths that met in the wide courtyard in front of the Keep. Two halves of a short stonewall bordered the courtyard and offered a place to sit in the sunshine Scotland normally saw too little of. The gap between the walls began the path down the center of the glen, which was kept clean of animal unpleasantness by older children being punished for various crimes.

There was one thing this clan had that others did not. No one knew from where it came, but an edict had been handed down from generation to generation. It demanded death to any man who intentionally hurt a woman or a child and each new laird swore to uphold it, including Laird Justin MacGreagor.

Well aware of the dangers women faced and that word of his daughter's attractiveness seemed on the lips of many men, Justin encouraged Paisley to wear some sort of covering on her head when she went outside. She saw no difference between being the only one with white hair and the only one wearing a scarf in summer, but to please him she wore one that hung down to her waist. It matched her green shirt and the new plaid she pleated and tucked under the wide leather belt her brother made for her. Yet she was not partial to wearing any headscarf at all and on this day, she would not have to.

It was indeed a special time in the MacGreagor Glen.

The long summer days were hot and when the crops were finally gathered and the storehouse filled to the brim, the MacGreagors invited members of other clans to a feast.

The women prepared every kind of food including salted fish and beef, yellow carrots, onions, turnips, peas and cabbage. None spared the ginger, pepper, nutmeg and saffron used to please even the most finicky palate. Breads of every kind were made from ground barley, oats, rye and wheat, and at this time of year the feast offered grapes, cherries, plums, apples, nuts, fruit pies and sweet breads. It was a feast fit for kings, soon to be spread out on tables in the courtyard for all to enjoy.

While the women prepared the meal, the men set out the necessary equipment for games in the grasses of the glen. They drove a wooden spike in the ground, marked the appropriate number of paces away from it and set horseshoes in a row to mark the last step a man could take before the toss. Other men brought out wooden targets, some round and some square to determine the best with a bow and arrows, while still more made ready the skills of strength by hauling out heavy logs. In the game, the men first lifted the log with two hands, balanced it on one and made sure it did not tip to one side or the other. The one who could hold it there longer than any other man would be the winner and it was this skill that challenged the men most. Lighter logs gave those not yet fully grown an equal chance to show their skill.

At last, the guests arrived and the games began. For the better part of two hours the men tested their skills, the women applauded or jeered and a panel of three elders announced the winners. The little children played their normal games of Stones for the boys and Queen of Scots for the girls, while the older boys tested their skills by sparring with wooden swords.

Because it was so hot, Justin opened the front and back door allowing a cool breeze to blow through his large, three-story home, and seated his guests at the long table in his colorfully decorated great hall. Not much had changed in this room over the years. One wall displayed old and new weapons of every sort while tapestries adorned the other walls. The long table remained in the middle of the large room together with tall-backed chairs and well-stuffed pillows of every color for guests to sit on. A large hearth at one end kept the place warm in winter and a back door led to a kitchen.

Paisley was not surprised to find herself sitting between Laird Haldane and Laird Graham so she could help her father entertain his guests. She smiled often, sat up straight and paid as much attention to one laird as the other. She even leaned forward often to include Laird Haldane's wife in the conversation.

Normally on hot days, the women braided their hair and some even piled it on top of their heads, but Paisley was often cold when others were comfortable. She knew the feast would continue into the evening and left her uncovered hair down, except for two small braids on the sides that she tied together with a green string in the back.

Paisley was surprised by her reaction to Laird Chisholm Graham. Even though she had seen him during his occasional visits before, it was never up close and never in a circumstance where she could talk to him. She found him charming, his manners impeccable and his smile oddly exciting. The others at the table talked, and loudly so, but sometimes it was as if no one else was in the room.

Once, when she looked into his fascinating amber eyes a little too long, she forced her attention to his necklace. It was made of leather and the odd shaped square held a collection of rubies and emeralds, with one large diamond in the middle. He wore his shirt open a little at the neck to show off his jewels and before she realized what she was doing, she reached up, brushed her hand against his skin and turned the necklace toward her for a better look.

The hair on his chest was the same golden brown as that on his head and face, she noticed, but when Paisley realized she had touched a man not her husband, she was horrified. She let go of his necklace, avoided his eyes and began a conversation with Laird Haldane on the other side of her.

As soon as the meal was finished and the air cooled, Laird MacGreagor and his guests went outside to join in the celebration. To the tune of the flute player's music in the courtyard, two women tried to teach two men how to dance a new sort of jig and everyone roared with laughter. The men did not seem to mind, although they occasionally stopped to glare at one jeer or another from the crowd. It seemed a hopeless case, but the men kept right on trying and soon others joined and tried to learn.

Laird Graham was never very far away from her and it pleased Paisley. It seemed to please him too, but he was a handsome man, yet unmarried and probably sought after by any number of women. It was always so for a laird, even the unsightly ones and Chisholm Graham was anything but unsightly. Just now, however, he seemed to be all hers and she lavished in his company. When she drifted away to gain a better view of the dancers, he drifted with her and when she next had something to remark upon, he was near enough to hear her and respond.

They laughed together, rolled their eyes at the same time, and when Laird Graham suggested they sneak a slice of honey bread out from under the watchful eye of a woman determined not to let the

children eat them all, she became a willing conspirator. It was not hard
to do, for a handsome man was admired by all women, no matter her
age, and while he distracted the unsuspecting woman, Paisley grabbed
the slice, walked away and went to the other side of the crowd. Soon
he was beside her, joined in her laughter and ate the stolen bread she
shared with him.

For Paisley, it was the most glorious evening of her life. Too soon,
the dancing ended, the visitors rode away and the MacGreagors settled
down for a good night's sleep. Years before, the second floor of the
three-story keep had been divided into two bedchambers and a sitting
room, but with six children, the sitting room became another
bedchamber for two of the boys. Paisley shared a room with her sister,
Leslie, until Leslie married and now their bedchamber was all hers.
Her father and mother occupied the third floor, but after Deora died
giving birth to her sixth child, Justin hardly spent any time there. Her
death was devastating to them all but in time he regained his good
humor, as did his children.

Yet it was at times such as this, Paisley wished she could share the
moment with her mother, or even her sister and perhaps stay up talking
far into the night. Alas, Leslie had a husband and there was no one to
talk to just now, so she looked out the window for a while longer and
then went to bed.

*

Laird Chisholm Graham lived less than an hour north of the
MacGreagors and an easy path took him and his six-man guard across
the river and through the narrow passageway between two hills. Once
that was accomplished, the first of three well-traveled paths took him

northwest toward home.

In the long days of summer, darkness fell for only a few hours a night, the horses knew the way and his men had consumed enough wine to make them less talkative.

Starting tomorrow, Chisholm guessed, his men would try lifting logs more often, so they could compete better the next time they were invited to join in the MacGreagor games. The thought made him smile. He remained considerably more sober than his men and with good reason -- a man, even a laird, could not hope to impress the woman he found fascinating with slurred words and improper manners.

Her smiles and laughter greatly pleased him and it wasn't long before he decided he wanted to see those smiles and hear that laughter far more often. The question was: how long should he wait before he went back?

*

A week later, Laird Graham had not come back and Paisley began to believe that instead of preferring her, he had only been pleasant for her father's sake.

Of her four younger brothers, one was far more enjoyable and sometimes far more bothersome than the other three. Justin named his eldest son Alisdair but the clan called him Sawney. He was the closest to her same age and seemed always to be in her way. Still, she was two years older and maintained at least a little control over him.

He was tall for his age and would likely be his father's same six feet, five inches by the time he was grown. He would look like Justin too, with dark hair and blue eyes, which would cause him to be sought after by women, if he ever managed to get beyond his awkward stage.

"God help the lass you marry," Paisley muttered as each step took them farther away from the village. Lately, Justin demanded that she not walk alone, even in the long, wide glen, for fear someone might take her, and this day, Sawney was her designated companion.

"I fear the same for your husband," Sawney said. He loved his sister and liked her too. She was often wise, usually even-tempered and did not mind answering his constant stream of questions. He saw nothing exceptional in her appearance, but if other men did, Sawney had no doubt she needed to be looked after. Every time he escorted her, it made him feel protective and all grown up.

"Sawney that is the third time you have bumped into me. Move over a pace or two."

He took two steps sideways and mockingly bowed. "As my lady wishes," he said in English instead of Gaelic.

Paisley rolled her eyes and kept walking. The spring flowers had come and gone, the morning was not yet too warm and the lower half of the glen held plenty of lush grass for their herd of horses to feed on. The cows grazed in an adjoining meadow and when she looked, the sheep were feasting on a faraway hillside.

Paisley's long shirt and pleated plaid were the same green as the trees in the forest except for the light blue threads woven between the green squares. On this day, she wore her matching scarf and new shoes that fit well.

"What, no argument?" Sawney asked. "Speaking English most often causes you great discomfort, though I cannot guess why."

She answered in English just to prove she could. "'Tis unnatural to speak it and I have yet to fully grasp why father makes us learn it still. Mother was English and often needed help with Gaelic words, but now that she has passed, the teaching is useless."

"You are right, as usual."

Paisley stopped walking and suspiciously eyed her brother. "What are you up to?"

"Nothing, nothing at all. Someday we might have a need, but I have said that many times and I suspect you tire of hearing it." He was up to something and decided he might as well get it over with. Sawney was growing so fast, the bottom of his kilt barely touched his knees and soon he would need a new pair of shoes with straps long enough to lace up his calves. "Sister, do you wish to marry?"

"Well, I would like very much to live in a cottage instead of the Keep where I must walk past all the lads to go outside." She sighed. "Father will not allow it until I take a husband, therefore I must marry."

Sawney clasped his hands behind his back and started them walking again. "But you would not marry just any lad, would you?"

"I'd not marry the candle maker that is certain. Nor do I fancy a lad without humor, wit or one who does not favor me often with a pleasant smile."

"I have heard Thomas fancies you."

She wrinkled her brow. "Which one? We have three lads named Thomas and four named William. Are there not enough other names?"

"The Thomas I mention is a hunter and a very good one at that. You would do well to let him court you, for many a lass thinks him handsome."

"Some call you handsome as well, it means nothing."

Sawney wasn't certain if he should be flattered or insulted. As they walked, he often looked at the others in the glen until he was sure he recognized them, but Paisley wasn't in any real danger there. Although there were trees easy to hide behind on both sides, MacGreagor guards were posted at short intervals so they could notify the clan of strangers, wild boars or any other danger. Fortunately, there had been no whistles signaling danger in weeks.

Paisley glanced at the corral where the stallions were kept away from the mares, noticed all the men watching her and chose to leave the path in favor of a row of logs on the opposite side of the glen. It was near the graveyard but it was her best choice. At least dead men did not gawk.

Beyond a sister, a new brother-in-law and four brothers, she had four sets of aunts and uncles and enough cousins to make a clan of their own. "Brother, do you always want to live here? I mean, I often wish we could just ride away and find a new home."

He smiled. "I doubt it would help. A bonnie lass is a bonnie lass no matter where she is, and lads will always want to look at her."

She sat down on a log and folded her arms. "I am cursed."

"If you must pity someone, pity me for I am my father's eldest son."

"Do you fear becoming Laird someday?"

"Fear it, nay. All the same, Father regrets it and so did Grandfather, I am told." He lifted his right foot and rested it on top of the log.

"If that be the case, once I am married we will encourage Father to ask the clan to choose another laird. Then he and all four of his sons can live in a small cottage like the rest of the people. Would you find that to your liking?"

"To spend more time with Father, I would live in a cart."

Paisley giggled. "Done then…as soon as I marry."

He returned her mischievous grin. "What shall Father become; a hunter, a guard or perhaps a tanner of hides?"

"I say we let him get his fill of fishing first. 'Tis that he loves most."

"As do I. An entire day fishing with Father without interruption, would be a dream come true, even if he demands we take my brothers with us."

"Would he truly relent though? I…"

Just then, a faint whistle at the small end of the glen interrupted them.

"Strangers," said Sawney. He stood up straight and reached out his hand. "To the forest, my lady." As soon as she got up, he hurried her across the graveyard, through the thick bushes and into the trees. Then they both laughed and relaxed.

Approaching strangers was not an uncommon occurrence, especially now with all the gossip about Paisley. At first, her father allowed men to meet her, but lately Justin wanted none of them to see her and Paisley was beginning to spend more time in hiding than anywhere else. Even when the women went to bathe in the loch, he dared not let her go. Instead, she used the bathing basin brought some years past from England. Nevertheless, she loved to swim and even the privilege of bathing in private seemed just another place to hide.

Often, when more than one red deer was shot, the meat was

placed in a pit, slow cooked for days and then shared by the entire clan. Herbs and spices made the otherwise tough meat tender, wine washed it down and the meal was again followed by dancing and singing to the music of the flute player. It was something they all looked forward to and the aroma that filled the air just now made Paisley hungry.

She did not care to even look at the strangers and assumed these were just more of the sort that came to gawk at her. What her father said to send them on their way, she did not know, nor did she care. They would be gone soon enough and that was all that mattered.

Careful to stay hidden, she leaned down, picked a forest flower and stood back up. Then she smelled it, peeked around the tree and caught her breath. The strangers numbered over twenty, a laird and his guard all dressed in matching white shirts with dark blue kilts. Each held his head high, rode his mount with pride and kept his weapons sheathed. Dark blue and white were the colors of the Grahams and when the man in the middle turned his face her way, her eyes lit up. "'Tis Laird Graham, he has come back!"

"So he has," said Sawney. The excitement in her voice was not lost on him and he suspected his friend, Thomas, would soon be sadly refused. Oh well, MacGreagor women were allowed to choose their own husbands and as painful as it was for MacGreagor men, that was the way it was.

She watched Chisholm ride all the way into the courtyard, dismount and go inside to greet her father. His return did not mean he preferred her and she was not sure if she should stay hidden, wait for Justin to send for her, or walk back into the glen where Laird Graham might easily find her.

Suddenly, an arm went around Paisley's waist, a hand clamped over her mouth and her eyes widened in horror. She dropped the flower and looked at Sawney, but he had troubles of his own. A second man had a firm grip on him and held the blade of a dagger to her brother's throat. She struggled to free her hand enough to pull her dagger, but when the man threatened to kill Sawney, she begrudgingly relaxed.

A second later, her attacker lifted her off the ground, hauled her up the hill and then hurried down the other side. Once they got to a horse, he abruptly let go of her, turned her around, hit her hard under the chin and knocked her out. Then he laid her over the back of the horse, untied the reins, mounted behind her and raced through the trees.

*

"Laddie, do not turn around or I will cut you ear to ear," the husky voice said in Sawney's ear.

For agonizing seconds, the older, stronger man kept his grip around Sawney's upper torso pinning his arms to his sides. Sawney could hear Paisley being taken away and had to do something even if it was wrong. He mustered all his strength, quickly put his right foot between his attacker's and looped it around a leg. Then he pulled hard. The warrior released him to regain his balance, stumbled and then fell on his backside. Sawney drew his sword as he spun around and quickly put the tip of it to the middle of the stranger's neck.

His eyes filled with rage and he wanted to kill the man. Instead, he put two fingers to his mouth and gave off the long, shrill whistle signaling danger. Not far away, a MacGreagor guard raced to his side and drew his own sword.

"Watch him, a lad took Paisley!"

"Sawney, you are bleeding!" Neasan shouted.

At a dead run, Sawney headed up the hillside and disappeared over the top, but by then, the man and Paisley were gone.

CHAPTER II

Justin was livid.

While men searched the woods on foot, Justin stood between Ginnion and Sawney with the tip of his sword against the stranger's throat. "Who has taken her?"

The stranger blinked repeatedly, but he did not answer.

"If you do not tell me I will kill you. Who did this?" Again his demands went unanswered. "You are willing to die? Who do you shield, a brother, a father?" Still, his captive said nothing.

"I will make him talk," said Ginnion.

Justin finally lowered his sword. "He is no use to us dead. Take him to the stable, set two guards outside and give him no food or water until he answers."

Justin watched Ginnion grab the man by the shirt, pull him to his feet and then shove him toward the glen. More men on horseback came to take up the search and Justin pointed the way, then he carefully examined Sawney's cut. Blood still ran down his son's neck and soaked into his shirt, but the injury did not appear to be deep and Justin was relieved. Still, a wound that did not heal could take a life.

"Father, please let me keep searching for her."

"The lads will find her. You are injured and I'll not lose a son *and* a daughter." Justin turned his son around and walked with him through the graveyard and across the grasslands to the path.

While the men searched, the women, children and elders gathered in the Glen silently watching, but a worried Sawney ignored them and kept looking back hoping to see the MacGreagor warriors bringing his sister back. It was not to be and in the end, his father took him up the path to the courtyard and the Keep.

Justin opened the door and followed Sawney inside. As he expected, the woman best at sewing wounds waited near the table with her cloths, needle and sinew.

*

The captured man wore a familiar red kilt and it wasn't hard to figure out the Kennedys had taken her. The Kennedys were known thieves and no one trusted them. Years before, another clan nearly annihilated the Kennedys over the theft of cows, and it had taken the Kennedys a long time to rebuild their numbers. Still, they were not half the strength of the MacGreagors.

For his Paisley, Laird MacGreagor would not hesitate to go to war. A few minutes earlier, he happily greeted Laird Chisholm Graham from the clan to the north, but now he ignored the man completely and waited for the woman to examine Sawney's neck. He watched her wipe the blood away twice before she assured him the boy did not need stitches.

Justin put his son into the care of his sisters, untied his sword and laid it on the table. Then he took his father's sword down off the wall and began to tie the strings around his waist. It was the same sword his grandfather, Kevin, used to execute two men and the one that killed Sween, his father's brother.

Often commented on by strangers who knew nothing about it, it was a very fine sword made of pounded iron, polished and sharpened on both sides to a thin edge. The weight was perfect for Justin's size and easily wielded from side to side when he used both hands. He hoped never to have to take it off the wall, but for his Paisley, he would gladly put it to good use.

Laird Graham stood in the middle of the room watching the rage grow in his friend's eyes. When the alarm sounded, Chisholm raced out the door right behind Justin, heard what had happened first hand and went to look for Paisley himself. Yet he was on foot and it was likely whoever took her had a horse. Then, when a second horse was found tied to a tree, he knew searching on foot was useless. He walked back over the hill and followed Justin and Sawney to the Keep. The only hope now was if the MacGreagors on horseback could pick up the trail in a forest that from the edge of the glen became increasingly dense.

"The MacGreagors and the Grahams have been friends for two generations," Laird Graham began, "What can we do to help?"

Justin barely heard Chisholm's words. Instead, he nodded to each of his most trusted men as they entered, four of whom were his brothers-in-law. "Shaw, I leave you in command. See that the women are kept out of the forest and keep my son to his bed for at least two days. His cut is not deep, but it may not heal if he is up and about."

"Aye," Shaw answered. He was nearly as big as Justin with the same dark hair and blue eyes, although his face was square and his beard longer than most men preferred.

Ginnion, the commander of the warriors, had never seen Justin so upset. "How many should prepare?"

He didn't mean to, but Justin turned his glaring blue eyes on his brother-in-law, "How many will it take to kill *all* the Kennedys?"

Taken aback, Ginnion drew in a long, deep breath and slowly let it out. He too was a very large man with a round face, blond hair and a touch of red in his beard and mustache. Justin MacGreagor was the most fair-minded man he had ever known and his laird's wrath would need to be tempered. Shaw knew Justin best, but Shaw was staying and Ginnion could only hope he had the wisdom to calm his laird down. "A hundred, perhaps."

"See to it." Justin made sure his sword rested correctly on his hip and then ran his fingers through his dark hair. "How soon can we leave?"

"Soon." Ginnion walked back out the door and was not surprised to find those not still combing the woods standing in the courtyard waiting. Each was a well-trained man with superior fighting skills and the choice of which to take was an easy one.

All over the village, women started to cry for fear of losing husbands, while the chosen warriors armed themselves for battle, kissed wives and children goodbye, and then headed down the glen to collect their horses. Just as Ginnion promised, soon, a hundred men and their Laird started down the glen toward the Kennedy village.

Behind them, Laird Graham got on his horse. He nodded to Shaw and casually led his much smaller band of men down the same path in the middle of the glen. He greatly admired Laird MacGreagor and earlier this day he hoped he and his men would be invited to partake in some of that sweet smelling venison. It was the last thing on his mind now.

A little more than a week ago, he sat next to Paisley at the feast. He wanted her, there was no doubt in his mind, but the MacGreagors allowed women to choose their own husbands and he had no idea how to win her affection. Such a thing was not required of a normal man in Scotland or in England. The man declared, the woman or more likely her laird agreed, and that was an end to it.

Chisholm had been home from the feast only a few days before he began to worry. The rumors of Paisley's beauty were sure to bring other lairds to see her and if Chisholm did not go back soon, he might be too late. Therefore, he set aside his duties as laird of a vast marketplace and set out to capture her heart the best way he could -- providing Justin MacGreagor would let him near his daughter again.

Now she was snatched away and try as he might, he could not imagine who took her. He turned his men up the path that led to the best place to cross the river and tried to think. The Kennedys were not the cleverest of men, perhaps, but they were certainly not stupid enough to take Laird MacGreagor's daughter. The MacGreagors were very large men with brute strength and none of the clans wanted to fight them.

When one man snatched a woman, he most likely wanted her for his own, but when men in numbers of two or more conspired, there had to be a larger plot. A laird was behind it, he guessed, but which one and why? At last count, there were at least three hundred clans in Scotland with more springing up every month. The Scots were a hearty bunch, often disagreed and just as often went off to find their own land and way of life.

Not as large as Justin, Chisholm was still an imposing figure of a man who had to fight another man two years earlier to gain the position of laird. His clan was nearly the same size as the MacGreagors and they also prided themselves on keeping fit. However, instead of being farmers or herders, most made leather goods and baskets of all shapes and sizes. Clans from all around came to barter and therefore, Chisholm hosted all the lairds, or at least most of them, at one time or another.

He kept his horse at a leisurely pace and his men knew not to interrupt his thoughts. Knowing other lairds personally gave him an advantage and he turned his attention to why someone would take her. Would she be held for ransom? If so, other than a beautiful daughter, what did Justin MacGreagor have that another laird badly wanted? He could think of nothing and when they crossed the river and then took the path to home, he decided to listen far more closely to the gossip. Someone knew something and he intended to find out what.

*

Justin's ride to the Kennedy hold was relentless, but Ginnion and the others managed to keep up. Occasionally, Ginnion glanced at his friend, saw Justin's jaw tense and then relax. It was the first time he noticed the gray along the sides of Justin's dark hair. The man was getting old and, he supposed, so was he. The father of five himself, he could imagine what was going through Justin's mind, and dared not think what he would do in the same circumstance. One thing was for sure, no matter how hard a man tried, he could not fully protect his children.

Ginnion's most immediate challenge was to keep Justin from killing Laird Kennedy, at least not before they had time to question him. He thought about getting in front of Justin as he should to protect his laird, but that might only irritate him more, so when the path narrowed to single file, he fell in behind. An hour passed and then another before they spotted smoke rising from the Kennedy village hearths.

At last, Justin put up his hand and slowed his warriors, yet he kept going and instead of telling his men to surround the village, he led the horde of well-armed, determined men down the path and into the center of the village.

Not nearly as particular as the MacGreagors, the Kennedy village had carts haphazardly parked halfway on and halfway off paths that had not been cleaned in a while. Milk cows munched on tall grass in front of cottages and chickens plucked at bits of grain that fell out of the cow's mouths. Some cottages were in need of repair while others appeared to have new thatched roofs. Like all clan holds, the cottages surrounded the courtyard and a one-story keep. People not already outside stepped out of cottage doors to watch the MacGreagors pass.

Alarmed by the thundering sound of so many horses, Laird Kennedy rushed out of his keep and stared at the invaders. "MacGreagor, what is it? What has happened?" Laird Kennedy demanded.

Justin swung down off his horse, drew his sword and walked forward until he was within an arm's reach of Laird Kennedy. "Give her back!"

"Give who back?"

"You are well aware of who."

Laird Kennedy was no longer a young man either, and the fury in

Justin's eyes caused him to take a step back and bump into one of the guards standing behind him. "I tell you true, I do not know…"

Justin raised his sword with both hands as if to strike and repeated his demand one more time. "Your lads took my daughter and I want her back. Give her to me or you will be the first to die!"

A much smaller man with red hair and an untrimmed beard, Laird Kennedy took another step out of Justin's reach and was grateful his guard had moved so he could. "We do not have her. Search if you will, but your daughter is not here. Why do you say we took her?"

Standing next to Justin, it was Ginnion who answered, "We caught one and he wears a Kennedy kilt."

"Has he a name?" Kennedy asked.

"He will not speak."

Kennedy turned his attention back to Justin. "Do you think me daft? What cause would I have to take her unless I wished to die a very painful death? I swear to you I sent no lads to do such a deed." He paused to think for a moment. "However, we are missing two kilts. I suspect you have been tricked, MacGreagor."

Justin's glare had not changed and it took time before he finally lowered his sword and looked away. When he looked back he was more placid, but not by much. "We must know for sure, let us search for her."

Laird Kennedy nodded. Instantly, Justin's men spread out and began methodically searching all the cottages. None of the people opposed the fierce MacGreagors and as the search began, Laird Kennedy walked to the door of his keep, opened it wide and let Ginnion go inside to look around. The great hall, with adjoining bedchambers and a kitchen, was easily searched. Save for the Laird's wife and children, no one was there. A few minutes later, Ginnion came back out, looked at Justin and shook his head.

Justin put his sword back in its sheath and started to rub his brow. In all his years, he had never faced anything like this and truly did not know what to do next. Could he search all of Scotland for her? He was willing, but he had a clan to think of and being away from them left him, as well as them, vulnerable.

"MacGreagor?"

Justin heard the voice, but couldn't quite make out what it was saying.

"MacGreagor, drink this. You look like death, not that I blame you, I have daughters of my own," said Laird Kennedy. He held the goblet out to Justin, watched him take it and down the contents. Then he recovered the goblet and took a deep breath. "One thing the Kennedys do well is spread gossip. Tell us what to say and we will begin it." He waited, but Justin went back to thoughtfully rubbing his brow.

"We could offer a reward for her recovery," Ginnion suggested.

"And a price on the head of the one who took her," Laird Kennedy added.

"Nay," said Justin seeming to gather his wits at last. "If he is in fear, he may hurt her...if he hasn't already."

"You are right, MacGreagor," said Kennedy. "What sort of reward? A high enough one will spread all over Scotland and everyone will look for her. A woman with white hair cannot be easily hidden."

Justin's fury instantly returned, "How do you know of her white hair?"

"Calm yourself, MacGreagor. I saw her last spring when I came to get my dog. Do you not remember?"

Justin ran his fingers through his hair and closed his eyes, "I have gone daft, finally."

Ginnion was beginning to breathe a little easier. Most of the men were back and Justin was calming down. "What reward can we offer?"

Justin spread his feet apart and folded his arms. "We have a jeweled chalice made of gold. Will that be enough to entice lads to find her?"

Kennedy raised an eyebrow. "Indeed, I am enticed to go look myself. Come inside, MacGreagor, and rest. If we put our heads together, perhaps we might think who took her. I would very much like to know who wanted you to accuse us."

*

Chisholm Graham was stumped. For the life of him, he could not think who would have taken Paisley. As far as he knew, there were no arguments over water, land or livestock; the normal reasons men went to war. Barely aware of where he was, he followed his men into the courtyard in front of his own keep and dismounted. He dared not think what his lovely Paisley was going through and pushed those thoughts completely out of his mind. She was not dead, he was certain of that much; it made no sense at all for anyone to take her just to kill her. No, there was some sort of intrigue afoot, but what?

There was the legend of a golden sword in Scotland, but why would anyone think Justin had it? According to the legend, it belonged to no specific clan, only a woman who could kill with a look. One version claimed a man who dared touch the sword would die and another said the King of Scots had it. Chisholm believed the latter was most likely true.

What then? Chisholm was about to enter his keep when an idea struck him. Perhaps there was a way to find her and he might not even have to leave his home to do it.

*

There was nothing more to discuss with Laird Kennedy and with no thought as to where to go next, Justin and his men went back to the MacGreagor glen.

Already, the Kennedys were spreading gossip about his daughter's abduction. A shout of, "Have you heard the news?" soon reached the MacDuff, the Swinton, the Haldane, the Macalister, the Gunn, the Keith and in another day it would reach the ears of the far away clans, and even the King of Scots. All Justin could do now was wait for some word of who had taken her.

Long into the night Justin walked the floor of the great hall trying desperately to understand what happened. He did not blame Sawney; he was still a boy and did the best he could. He was glad Sawney's cut was not worse than it was, but what of Paisley and why was the protection cast around her not enough?

As soon as it was late enough and he was certain the rest of the clan was asleep, he picked up a holder with a lit candle and went out the door. He cupped his hand around the flame, chose a path leading west and walked down the path until he came to an empty cottage. The door creaked when he opened it and he anxiously glanced around to see if anyone noticed. The guards were far enough away not to recognize him, none of the doors on the opposite side of the path opened and a candle in the dark was not all that uncommon.

Justin eased inside, slowly closed the door and set the candle on the table. He ignored the cobwebs and the dust, knelt down beside the wall and wiggled two stones free. Once he had them on the floor, he felt inside the hiding place until he located a cloth sack. Gently, he pulled it out, untied the strings that held the sack closed and widened the mouth. Then he reached in and withdrew a solid gold chalice with diamonds, rubies and opals imbedded in the sides.

"Thank you, Aunt Jessup," he whispered. She was not his true aunt and in fact, was English instead of Scottish. Nevertheless, she married three times into the MacGreagor clan before she passed at the age of 63. Always feisty and full of life, Jessup was once wealthy in her own right and a good friend to the King of England, who bestowed upon her many wonderful gifts. This chalice was one of them.

She liked to laugh over the toil it took getting her wealth into Scotland only to find the MacGreagors had little use for such things. Even so, items from her coffers bought several English brides at a time when Scottish brides were scarce. Naturally, Justin, being the son of Laird Neil MacGreagor, was the only one she told about the treasure. Jessup liked to look at them and when Justin came to visit, she never failed to drag everything out and show him.

Now, Jessup was helping him try to save his daughter. He quietly put the sack back inside the wall, replaced the stones and tucked the chalice inside his shirt. He picked up the candle, opened the door and retraced his steps to the great hall.

CHAPTER III

Justin MacGreagor was not the only one who lost sleep that night. Alone in his second floor bedchamber, Chisholm let the window curtain down to darken the room, undressed and climbed into bed. Every once in a while, a breeze lifted the edge of the curtain to let in the light and he was reminded the room needed decorating.

His bedchamber was pleasant enough with a bed, small table and chairs, and two trunks against the wall that kept his valuables and his extra clothing clean. Yet no color brightened the stonewalls and the dark blue of his plaids did nothing to help.

Chisholm's idea was to start a rumor and offer a reward higher than any ransom could be, but he suspected he had little that was valuable enough to tempt a man. He had a handful of jewels and the ones in his necklace, which he would gladly give up, but would it be enough?

Other than adornment, he had not been all that fond of his jeweled necklace, but at the MacGreagor feast Paisley seemed to admire it. When she touched his chest to turn the necklace toward her, it greatly surprised him -- pleasantly so. There were women in his past, but never had the touch of any other affected him as much as hers and he could not seem to get it out of his mind.

Several times, he closed his eyes and tried to sleep, but the image of her face and what might be happening to her haunted him. Again, he tried to guess what the MacGreagors had that another laird wanted that badly. At last, sleep overcame him and he rested both body and mind for a few hours.

*

Paisley woke up in a bed not her own with a headache the likes of which she had never known. At first, she believed her jaw was broken, but slowly moving it up and down proved her wrong. Nevertheless, the pain was excruciating and it was all she could do to make herself sit up. At least she was alone, still had her clothes on and didn't hurt anywhere else.

At length, she examined the contents of the room. Nothing looked familiar, although the bedchamber was lavishly furnished just as she imagined a king's castle to be. Perhaps being the daughter of a laird spoiled her, but she did not care much for fancy furnishings.

It was an odd shaped room, long and narrow, rather than wide. The head of the bed was against the wall in the middle of the room, leaving just enough space at the foot to walk around it. A table with two chairs had been placed at each end of the room with matching trunks between them and the bed. Works of art, the sort she heard the English preferred, hung on the walls and they were not nearly as wonderful as the tapestries that adorned her father's keep.

There was a door at one end, but when she spotted a window at the other end, she got up and walked to it. Perhaps she could tell where she was by looking out the window, but her eyes were not focusing well and she had to grab hold of the back of a chair to steady herself.

She abruptly remembered what happened, including the face of the man who hit her and worst of all, the knife being held to her brother's throat. Paisley bowed her head and said a silent prayer for Sawney's survival. She crossed herself in the Catholic tradition and decided she could see well enough after all.

As soon as she made it to the window, she drew in a sharp breath. She was much higher up than she imagined. Timidly, Paisley inched closer to the window, stuck her head out just enough and peeked down. Three identical windows were in a row below her. "Four floors?"

"Aye," said a voice behind her.

Paisley turned around, nearly lost her balance and was grateful when the man reached out to take her arm and steady her. He was not the man who hit her and she found that disappointing. One moment with her long fingernails stuck in his eye would make her feel much better.

"Who are you?"

"I am Laird Macalister."

"Why have I been taken?" she demanded. He looked truly concerned but he did not speak. Instead, he used his other hand to pull the scarf off her head and admired her loosely braided white hair.

"I have heard of your beauty and the rumors are all true."

"You are too late, I am married."

He smiled and let go of her. "It matters not."

She reached for her dagger, found it missing and glared at him instead. "It will matter when my husband finds you."

He went to the nearest table, picked up a pitcher and poured liquid into a goblet. "I am sorry my lad hit you, but it was the only way to keep you from screaming." He offered her the goblet and when she refused, he shrugged and set it on the table. "Tis only wine for your headache. You may scream all you want here; no one will hear you. Are you hungry?" It didn't surprise him when she shook her head. "Perhaps later, then."

"Why did you take me?"

"Do not concern yourself, you are here and here you will stay until I say otherwise." He started for the door.

"Where is here?"

He paused at the door and turned to politely answer her question. "You are yet in Scotland, but your father will never find you here. You will be well treated and no further harm will come to you, of that I give my pledge."

As soon as he closed the door behind him, she heard a slight screeching noise and then heard a heavy lock bar fall into its holder. She stared after him for a moment, decided he probably didn't put poison in the wine and grabbed the goblet off the table. Opening her mouth wide enough hurt, but she managed to drink it down. It took but a few seconds to begin to warm her stomach and work its magic on her headache, but it was bitter and the taste lingered.

Paisley poured herself another goblet full, pulled a high-backed chair away from the table and sat down. At length, she put her elbows on the table, her head in her hands and let the tears flow.

Not but a few moments later, the bar lifted on the lock and the door opened once more. Paisley wiped her tears, turned and was surprised to see a woman bringing her a bowl of food. Until then, she had not realized how hungry she was and she'd forgotten all about the venison left behind.

"I am Rona, Mistress."

For the life of her, Paisley did not understand why she called her mistress, but she let it slide. "Where am I?"

"Home, Mistress."

Suspicious, Paisley eyed the much shorter woman with red hair and brown eyes. "Home where precisely?"

"Where you are to be married." Rona spotted the bruise under Paisley's chin and winced. You took a bad fall, Mistress. Perhaps you will remember when you have rested.

"I did not fall; I was hit and snatched away."

"I see." Rona walked to the bed and began to straighten the blankets. "Eat, Mistress, you need to keep up your strength. 'Tis beef broth and bread, easy to chew with an injury such as yours. Laird Macalister thought to ask for beef since you do not prefer mutton."

Perplexed, she wrinkled her brow. "How does he know I do not like mutton?"

Rona was finding the conversation unsettling, finished making the bed and walked to the door. "He said you would not remember." She opened the door, walked out and replaced the lock in its holder.

Laird Macalister stood waiting for Rona in the hallway and after she curtsied, she lowered her voice. "'Tis just as you said, she claims to be snatched away."

He looked disappointed and whispered back, "She thinks she is already married, too."

Rona shook her head in sorrow and disappeared down the hallway. At least going down three flights of stairs would be easier than climbing up with a bowl in her hands.

Behind the closed door, Paisley stared at the globs of bread soaked in the broth. She would have preferred a more fitting meal for morning, but she had little choice. She touched the liquid with her finger, tasted it, found it sufficiently salted and sat down to eat.

*

Shaw was quiet when he entered the great hall and found Justin with his head on the table sound asleep. Justin's hand was wrapped securely around the stem of the most beautiful chalice Shaw had ever seen. Years ago Shaw married Justin's sister, knew every inch of the village and could not imagine where Justin had that hidden. He quietly sat down and just stared at the jewels and the pure gold chalice.

A moment later, Ginnion entered and was just as astonished. "I thought he lied," he whispered to Shaw, taking a chair opposite him.

Trying not to wake his laird, Shaw only nodded. A few minutes later, the room was filled with men being as quiet as mice and staring at the chalice as the rising sun filtered in through the high windows and made the gold shimmer.

At last, Justin woke up, held his hurting neck and lifted his head. He looked at Shaw first, "Have they found her?"

Shaw swallowed hard and shook his head. "We have had no word but it is early. What would you have us do this day?"

Taking pity on his laird, Ginnion got up, walked behind Justin and began to massage his neck and shoulders. "The lads want to search for her. They suggest they split up, spy on the other clans and perhaps they might see something. Perhaps they might even see Paisley."

The massage was just what he needed and Justin closed his eyes. "It is sound thinking, far more sound than my thinking at the moment.

Did Laird Graham leave?"

"Aye, right after you," Shaw answered. "He was not a happy lad."

"Send a messenger to say I did not mean to slight him."

"That was not what upset him."

Shaw suddenly had Justin's full, alert attention. "What then?"

"He came to ask for Paisley."

"Did he say as much?"

"Nay, it was his second in command who told me."

"Do second in commands often gossip about their lairds?"

It was the first smile anyone had seen since Paisley was taken. "I know I do," admitted Shaw.

Justin couldn't help but crack a smile. "You are a good lad, Shaw MacGreagor." He lifted the chalice and handed it to him. "Take it outside and show it to everyone. When they are asked if I have such a thing, they can say they saw it for themselves."

Shaw nodded, took the chalice and went out the door.

Abruptly, Ginnion grabbed hold of Justin's chin, sharply jerked his face to the side and popped his neck. Then he came around to face his laird to see if he was about to be killed.

"I was not expecting that, but I thank you, Ginnion."

All at once, three boys scurried down the stairs and rushed to their father. "Is Paisley back?" the youngest wanted to know. When Justin admitted she was not, the eight-year-old hung his head and went into his father's arms for comfort.

Justin looked up at Hew, his second eldest son. "How is Sawney?"

"He wants to get up and vows to kill me if I do not let him. I said I would ask you, which made him lie back down. That laddie is a horse's behind, Father."

The other men snickered and Justin frowned. "Do you not mean a mule's behind? A mule is far more stubborn."

"Aye, a mule's behind."

"Go tell the servers we are hungry." He turned the boy in his arms around and nudged him toward the kitchen door.

"Very well, father, but next time make Hew go tell them, it is his turn."

Justin rolled his eyes. "I forgot."

Hew waited until his little brother was out the door before he asked, "Can I go look for Paisley? I know all her hiding places."

"Son, if she got away, she would have come home, but I suppose it will not hurt to look."

Forgetting his morning meal, Hew ran out the door and closed it too hard behind him. An instant later, he stuck his head back inside. "Sorry, Father." Then he was gone again.

Justin glanced at the men watching him. "She might have gotten free. If only we knew which way he took her."

Ginnion was also married to Justin's sister, only to the eldest one, Ceanna. "The lads need to help, let them search the forest again. Perhaps she has gotten lost trying to get back." He was pleased when Justin nodded.

With the other men following, he led the way out the door to give the men their assignments. If anyone knew the forest, he did and the thought of his niece out there alone and lost and alone bothered him greatly. Men were not the only danger for a woman in Scotland.

As soon as they were gone, Justin went upstairs to check on his son. He quietly opened the door, peeked in and found his son wide awake, but still lying down.

Sawney nearly had tears in his eyes when he spoke, "I have shamed myself, Father, I did not protect her."

Justin pulled up a chair and sat beside the bed. First, he wanted to look at the wound and satisfy himself. The blood on the outside of the cloth was dry, and when he lifted the loose bandage, he decided the two-inch cut was healing. "I shamed myself by not protecting a woman once."

Sawney put his legs over the side of the bed and sat up. "Truly?"

"Aye, she was your mother. I did not forgive myself for many months after."

"Did someone hurt her?"

"Aye, but 'tis a long story best saved for later. I vowed it would never happen again, but as you see, I did not keep my daughter safe."

"But Father, you were not even there when Paisley was taken."

"True, but I should have had a lad watch over her, not a laddie. The fault is mine."

Sawney lowered his eyes. "I did not think anyone brave enough to get so close to the glen. We were watching Laird Graham; I did not hear anyone and I did not think to look behind us."

"My father told of a child who once snuck up behind the warriors and pinched them. It made the men more aware and instead of punishing the child, the laird encouraged it. Perhaps we should let your brothers do the same."

Finally, Sawney smiled, "My brothers would like nothing better."

Justin tenderly mussed his son's hair and stood up. "Stay in bed until the evening meal, then you may come down."

"Thank you, Father."

*

Justin climbed the second flight of stairs to his bedchamber. It didn't help to remember what happened to Deora so long ago, so he pushed it out of his mind. He did not enjoy being in his bedchamber without her either so he looked for clean clothing, gathered them and went back down to the great hall.

When he arrived, he felt even worse. His eldest daughter, Leslie, was there with tears in her eyes and he hadn't bothered to go to her cottage to comfort her. He set his clothing on the table, wrapped his arms around her and kissed the top of her dark hair. "Forgive me; I believe I have gone daft."

"As have I." She pulled away and looked up into his eyes. "I am with child."

Truly delighted, he hugged her again. Of all his children, this one looked the most like her mother with dark hair and blue eyes. "Now there's a spot of good news. Are you well?"

She wiped the tears off her cheeks with her hand and stayed in his arms a while longer. "They tell me in about seven months, I will be."

Justin chuckled. "Come sit down, have you eaten?"

"Aye, but it did not stay down long. Father, where can Paisley be? I fret over her so."

He pulled out a chair and let her sit down. "We all do. You are often with her, have you noticed strangers in the woods or any lad paying particular attention to her?"

"I have seen nothing odd." Justin looked even older than the day before and she noticed. "What can I do to help?"

"You can see your brothers stay out from underfoot. I've not the restraint for them just now. And, you can come with me to the loch. I wish to bathe, but not if the lasses are still there."

She stood back up. "Most of the lasses are back, but I will go with you just in case some of them linger."

*

The Graham village was close to the edge of the massive forest that covered most of southern Scotland. It looked much like many other villages, except for the excess of baskets stored in a large three-walled shelter to keep them out of the rain. They had other storehouses too, one to stock with food for winter and one that belonged to their Laird alone. The clan was composed of several hundred all, including the children, wearing matching colors, as was the custom in all clans.

The Keep was only two stories, yet expansive enough to house half the clan should a harsh winter and not enough fuel for hearths force them to double up. The cottages surrounded the Keep, paths enabled prospective customers to enter the courtyard from any direction and a nearby loch supplied them with water.

The baskets were hand crafted and made out of heather, an overabundant bush that grew wild. The people also made brooms, cloth sacks and of course, everything that could be made of leather.

For leather, they needed a large herd of cattle and making use of the hides supplied them with plenty of fresh meat. The excess beef was dried and smoked, and bartered in the marketplace in exchange for fresh fruits and vegetables. Occasionally, a price that seemed excessive caused an argument, but Grahams were prepared and usually tossed the buyer out of the village on his ear. Yet the Grahams also had a soft spot in their hearts and normally let the buyer back in, slipped food to a child that looked hungry and often accepted worn out or useless goods from widows.

The most popular items were weapons and leather sheaths. Laird Graham bartered for the weapons from another clan, but his clan made the sheaths and many thought the workmanship the finest in the world.

More importantly, the Graham market was a splendid place to hear all the latest gossip, for which buyer and seller alike had an insatiable appetite.

Over all this, Chisholm Graham was laird. His home was clean and well kept, but like his bedchamber, it desperately needed a woman's touch. For that he had plenty of bartered tapestries and adornments in his storehouse for his bride to choose from, should he finally have a bride. He was nearly twenty-three and could have taken a wife earlier, but there was never enough time to go looking, and choosing one from his own clan, most lairds knew, was problematic at best. Women had a way of not showing the proper respect to one they grew up with and perhaps did not like.

Besides, he wanted a wife who loved him the way his mother loved his father. Marriage was forever and life without love could be brutal. It was not until he laid eyes on Paisley at the MacGreagor feast that he knew it was fortunate he had not already taken a wife. Yet if the MacGreagors could not keep her safe, how was he to?

It was of that he thought as he sat outside on an aging but comfortable trunk. He reasoned that if he managed to find and marry her, he would hold the biggest wedding feast in all of Scotland and let men get their fill of looking at her. Then they would know the most enchanting woman of all was his and his alone. Perhaps he would even invite the King and Queen.

When he wasn't thinking of her, he watched the people come and go and listened intently to the gossip. The rumor of Justin's missing daughter and the unbelievable reward he offered for her return came to the Graham marketplace quickly. He had no idea Justin had that kind of wealth and it made his assortment of jewels seem like a pitiful offer in comparison. He wondered if Justin had a lot more wealth than he wanted anyone to know. Ransom, therefore, was not out of the question after all.

On the other hand, was a gold chalice something an ordinary man would risk his life to get? Perhaps Chisholm had something of value to offer too, something the common man wanted even more than gold and jewels -- something that would help feed his family and his clan.

He quickly stood up, climbed on top of the chest and shouted, "Silence!"

Normally on guard to keep the peace, his men stared at the Graham laird who had never done such a thing before. Realizing he was serious, they quieted the crowd.

"Justin MacGreagor's daughter is missing. To the lad who brings her to me, I will give four cows and a bull." He could tell by the shock on their faces they considered it a fortune.

Twice more that morning as new barterers arrived, Chisholm made the same announcement. When they heard it, two brothers in the back of the crowd exchanged looks. "Five head," Adair MacDuff whispered to his brother, Ross.

*

The silence was deafening in the place Paisley now considered a stuffy and rotting castle. She was too high up to hear the villagers and she could detect no footsteps outside her door. Why anyone would intentionally live in a place like this was beyond her. The furnishings were indeed as grand as any she had ever seen, but the place smelled of mold. The dry season was upon them, the heat on the fourth floor was stifling and she wanted nothing more than to somehow climb down and run to the shade of the nearest tree. Even a breeze would help, but with only one window, a cross wind was impossible.

Climbing down was an idea she constantly toyed with. She even wondered if a jump would break both of her legs. Perhaps she could tie the covers together, she thought, but when she examined them, the cloth looked worn through and unreliable. She would be better off jumping.

For long moments, she stood at the window and scanned the countryside. Nearest to her were scant trees, a grassy yard and beyond that, tilled land in uneven squares of green, blue and yellow according to the crop. Farther away, she could see meadows, rolling hills and mountains the size of which she had never seen before. Another time, she would have loved sitting in the window just to look at them.

There seemed to be few people, although she spotted one woman on a stool that morning milking a cow and squirting a share of milk into a waiting cat's mouth. She kept watch and hoped the woman would glance her direction so she could wave a desperate wave for help. Alas, when she finished milking, the woman carried the bucket out of sight without as much as an upward tilt of her head.

Paisley sighed and once more sat down at the table. She could not be certain, but she guessed her father was sending word of her abduction all over Scotland. It was with this in mind that she removed her scarf, unbraided her hair and pulled it around to the front to let it show the next time she went to the window. Maybe, just maybe someone might see her even if she could not see them. It was the first time ever she was glad to have such distinguishing hair.

As soon as she heard someone begin to unlock her door, she quickly retied her scarf and was ready to pounce no matter who it was. The instant the door swung open, a rush of cool, refreshing air reached her. She basked in the feeling a moment more before she realized her guest was a boy of not more than five. "Thank you."

"For what," the child asked.

"For letting in the pleasant air. 'Tis far too hot in here." Her impulse was to run right over the child, find the stairs and flee for her life, but the little boy's smile was overwhelming and her heart melted. A few moments with a child would make no difference, she decided, so she walked to him, knelt down and opened her arms. Instantly, he went into them and kissed her cheek.

"Shall you be my mother, then?"

Paisley got up, carried him to the bed and settled him in her lap. He left the door open and at least she could enjoy the breeze. "Where is your first mother?"

"In the ground."

"I see." She had never heard it put just that way and it surprised her, although with four younger brothers, it shouldn't have. "My mother is in the ground too."

"Are you sad?"

"Very sad. Is Laird Macalister your father?"

He nodded. "Father is a very big lad and fierce when I am bad."

"My father is the same."

"I like you, shall you be my mother? Oh please say you will."

"I cannot promise. You see, I am lost and my father does not know where I am."

"Lost?"

She had to do something soon before the open door was discovered. She decided to set the boy beside her on the bed and make a run for it, but it was too late for when she looked up, the figure of Laird Macalister stood blocking the doorway. Paisley turned away and closed her eyes. "There now, that's a good laddie. Best you go along so I may speak to your father."

In a blink, the child hopped down, skirted around his father and ran down the hallway to the stairs. She listened, and tried to count the sound of his shoes on the steps, but Macalister's voice interrupted her.

"That was very kind of you."

She stood up and turned her glare on him. 'Tis too hot up here! You promised no further harm would come to me, yet you let me bake like bread in a kiln." Her ire did not seem to faze him at all.

"Why did you not try to run?"

"What do you intend to do with me? Do you hope to ransom me for some imaginary wealth?"

He left the door wide open and walked to the window. "I would prefer you not take your scarf off while standing at the window."

His back to her, Paisley glanced at the open doorway and tried to guess if she could outrun him. Probably not, especially since she did not know which way to run. No doubt he had guards on the stairs prepared to capture her anyway. Perhaps the best answer was to let him gain some measure of trust in her.

"Did you hear me?" he asked as he turned around to face her.

"Aye." It was the first time she took a really good look at him. His face was not an unpleasant one, his build was acceptable and his manner of speaking did not frighten her. Still, he was not Chisholm and it was of Chisholm she dreamed since the day she sat next to him at the feast. Indeed, Macalister was nothing more than a corrupt, evil man with yellow hair and dull brown eyes. He was the one man she could never love.

"We are to wed soon. Rona will come to help you change into Macalister colors."

"I need to bathe, I smell of horse sweat, not to mention my own."

He looked down at the floor and considered how she managed to change the subject. It was an acquired trait and one he greatly admired. Paisley was as clever as he had heard. "As you can see, I have no need of your father's wealth or that of any other man. You will marry me and you will be happy here."

"I will be happy when my father kills you and burns this rotting castle to the ground!"

This time he narrowed his eyes, but just for a moment before he smiled. "He will never find you here and once we are married, it will be too late."

Paisley looked away. He was right; once she was married, even her father could not set it aside. Never had she felt so trapped. "I will not agree to marry you and the priest will not force me."

Macalister walked straight to her and looked deep into her eyes. "I have seen your tender heart and you will do it for my son, if for no other reason. You will also do it to keep me from killing Rona." The shock in her eyes was complete and he was certain his threat was well understood before he left her and walked to the door.

"Can you not leave the door open? Post your guard if you must, but do not make me suffer the heat." She watched him leave it open and heard him open the door to the room across the hall. The burst of cooler air rushed to her and she took a forgotten breath. Then she heard his footsteps on the stairs and counted them. Once it was quiet again, she walked to the window. Someone told him she let down her scarf, which meant there were few in his clan she could trust. If she could escape, though, which way was best to go?

Quietly, she walked to the open door and peeked down the hall in both directions. Seeing no one, she scooted across, went into the bedchamber and hurried to the window opposite hers. There it was, finally, the forest she loved and beyond the forest, the people she loved.

Paisley looked down, studied the courtyard and counted the number of cottages between the courtyard and the forest, and then quickly went back to her bedchamber before she was discovered. She sat on the bed and tried to think of a way to get down the stairs and out the door without being seen.

Suddenly, she caught her breath. Was this the same Macalister suspected of killing his wife and three daughters in a fit of rage?

CHAPTER IV

Justin might have thrown the man out of the great hall had he not been the most influential man in Scotland, not counting the king. Laird Monro's land was vast, his clan numbered in the thousands and he was not above burning a village down to get what he wanted.

Justin and his advisors were trying to decide where to look for Paisley next when the whistles announced strangers. As soon as Laird Monro and his small army of men arrived in the glen, Justin rushed to his third floor bedchamber window to see if he could spot Paisley among them. There was a woman with them, but it was not his daughter and he was so disappointed his shoulders slumped.

All day his men searched the woods, spied on the closest clans, including the Kennedys just in case, and returned with nothing to report. Their captive still wasn't talking and it was all Justin could do to keep his temper under control. He was exhausted, worried, enraged and the last thing he needed was to entertain uninvited and unwanted guests.

By the time he went back down stairs, Laird Monro and the woman were standing in front of Shaw and Ginnion in the great hall. The woman curtsied and he nodded his appreciation. She was not an unsightly woman, though a bit too thin. Her hair was a light yellow, her eyes were a gray-blue and her smile was pleasant.

Laird Monro was the exact opposite. He was rotund, had red hair, breathed heavy and his voice boomed across the room. "She is my daughter, she needs a husband and I choose you!"

Justin took a step back. "I have no want of a wife."

Laird Monro took a step closer. "Does she displease you?"

Justin blinked twice and tried to choose his words as carefully as he could. "If I was in want of a wife, she would please me but I am not. And just now…"

"Then you will want her later, MacGreagor. I know of your missing daughter and perhaps any other time, you might be good-natured. I intend to leave my daughter with you until I return and by then you will want her."

Justin began to rub his brow again, a habit he had only just begun the day before. "We will be pleased to see to her comforts, but…"

"Good." Laird Monro handed a heavy sack to Justin and started for the door. "If you bed her before marriage, I will kill you." With that, he walked back out the door and slammed it behind him.

His daughter jumped. Then she closed her eyes and bowed her head. She listend to her father shout orders and then heard the sound of horses as he and his army headed back down the glen. Only then did she have the courage to raise her head again, but instead of anger, she saw compassion in Justin's eyes. "I know not what to say."

"How have you heard of my missing daughter?"

"We heard it on the paths."

"Good, then I am assured it is spreading."

"You will be happy to know we heard it not once but three times since yesterday noon." She watched Shaw relieve Justin of her sack and continued, "I thank you for letting me abide with you for a time.

God knows I can use a rest from my father's unpleasantness."

He had not expected her honesty or her kind nature. It was as if she wanted to put him at ease. "Have you a name?"

"I am Blanka and a forced marriage pleases me even less than it pleases you." She walked to Shaw, took her sack and then stood back. "Have you an empty cottage?"

Justin looked to Shaw first and then to Ginnion. Any other time, he would know the answer to that question, but he was not thinking clearly.

"She must stay here," Ginnion said.

"Why?" Justin asked.

"People talk and if Laird Monro thinks you have thrown her out…"

Justin puffed his cheeks. "You are right, but the only place of privacy is Paisley's bedchamber."

Shaw guessed the idea of was painful for his laird and took pity. "We will bring in a second bed and Paisley's bed will stay in wait for her return. Do you agree?"

Justin hesitated before he finally nodded. "Shaw, go get Leslie. She can settle Blanka and show her where to bathe. The water is warm and…" He stopped in mid-sentence. "Do you swim?"

She finally smiled, "Only as often as I can."

"Then you will be happy here."

"Laird MacGreagor I know you need not have me to bother over at a time such as this. My father is often…well he often does not consider the troubles of others, only the desires of his own heart. Lately, he desires to be shed of me, it seems." She did not mean to make the men pity her, but the words just came out that way.

"Come sit down," Justin said. "You are not a bother to us. He urged her to sit at the table and poured her a goblet of water. He nodded for both Shaw and Ginnion to carry out his orders and then took a seat at the head of the table. He truly hated being distracted and it didn't take long for his thoughts to return to finding Paisley

Blanka did not interrupt the troubled man, sipped her water and waited while Shaw and Ginnion found a bed and had it moved up the stairs. Soon after, Leslie came with an armload of bedding and took Blanka up the first flight of stairs to her rest.

"Marriage to her would be a good match," Shaw whispered as soon as Blanka was out of hearing. A connection between our two…"

Justin stood up and glared. "Then you marry her!"

"I already have a wife and I fear your sister more than I do you," said Shaw

Ginnion couldn't help but chuckle and soon faced another of Justin's glares. "He is right, 'tis time you remarried, the clan needs a mistress and your sons need a mother."

"How can you speak of this now? Where is my daughter? Send the lads out again; surely there is gossip by now."

"Tis but the second day and this one not yet complete," Shaw shot back. "We must wait."

"Aye, a new day of my daughter's misery." Once more Justin sat down at the head of the table and put his head in his hands. "I fear what is happening to her."

Shaw went to the table and poured his laird a goblet of wine. "It could be vengeance, who have we upset lately?"

It was a new thought and Justin immediately perked up. "Who?"

At almost the same time, Shaw sat on one side of the table while Ginnion took a seat on the other. "No doubt nearly every lad who came to see her," said Ginnion. "You have not allowed her to be seen in weeks, therefore, it is possible one might have been unduly upset by your denial."

"Did any of them seem upset?"

Shaw rolled his eyes. "All of them seemed upset. They rode long distances to see her and you denied them."

"Do you mean I should have put my daughter on display?"

Ginnion shook his head, "I would not have."

"I thought once you denied a few, the rest would stop coming," said Shaw.

"So did I." Ginnion agreed. "It did not work; we Scots are stubborn lads."

Justin sipped his wine. Having even the smallest clue to who took her made his eyes brighten considerably. "Who came before Chisholm Graham?"

For hours, they recalled the clan names and tried to decide which was most annoyed. They were so intent in their discussion, they almost completely ignored Justin's four sisters, two more husbands, Sawney, who was finally allowed out of bed, and Blanka when she came down to partake in the evening meal. So they would not be bothersome, the younger children were sent to the kitchen to eat.

Normally a happy chatting family, this night each remained stoic and let the three men at the head of the clan keep talking. But Patches, Justin's youngest sister, could not hold her thought any longer. "Send a lass to search."

"What?" Justin asked.

Under the table, she took hold of her husband's hand to prepare for her brother's wrath if the idea enraged him. "Brother, we have lasses from nearly every clan married into ours. Instead of spying on the clans, send a lass back to see her family and look around. She can discover far more from inside than the lads can from without."

"And her husband with her?" Justin asked.

"Aye, her husband and two others," Shaw added. "If Paisley is found, she will need protection on the way back."

Justin got up, went to his sister and took her hand. Smiling a genuine smile at last, he helped her stand and took her into his arms. "Finally, you have become useful." Amid the giggles and chuckles of the others, he kissed her forehead and let her sit back down.

Blanka had not been shy a day in her life, yet she hesitated. Gathering her courage by the time Justin sat back down at the head of the table, she said, "Laird MacGreagor, might I say a word or two?" She waited for Justin's nod and began, "As you are well aware, there are several clans between your land and ours. My father insisted we stop at each, hoping to find a willing husband for me."

As the words left Blanka's lips, her embarrassment was evident on her face. Still, she forced herself to continue, "Always when my father enters a great hall, lairds are alarmed, yet I recall two who were more so than the others. Laird Gunn's tremble was so great, I pitied the lad." She stopped, wondering just how upset Justin would be when she mentioned the other name.

"Laird Gunn and who else?" he asked, trying to be patient with her.

Blanka lowered her gaze, "Laird Macalister."

The women in the room gasped. It was the worst name she could have brought up and it was all Justin could do to keep from standing up and beginning to pace. It took a moment to calm himself enough to ask, "What did Macalister do?"

"He claimed to be betrothed."

Noticing Justin gritted his teeth, Shaw took over the conversation. "Did he say the name of his bride?"

"Nay, but he did say they were to marry in a week's time."

Ginnion, normally the more calm of the three, questioned her further. "Why did you think that suspicious?"

"Father demanded to meet her and Macalister said she had not yet arrived."

"When was that?" Ginnion asked.

Blanka had to think for a moment. "We saw the MacDuff next, then Laird Kennedy and then we came here. So it must have been only two days, perhaps three. Aye, it was two nights and..."

Ginnion was starting to get as upset as his laird. "Is there more?"

She took a long breath and let it out. "Though he did not speak, there was a lad with Macalister. The lad stared at me and slightly shook his head as if to warn me of something. The window coverings were oddly let down for that time of day and it was difficult to see him, but there was also an elder lad in the great hall. He was made to no longer see."

"Do you mean someone blinded him?" asked Shaw.

"Aye, he had horrid scars around his eyes and I had to look away.

I was pleased when Father took me out. Macalister's castle is a dreadful place. It smells."

"Macalister," Justin turned to Shaw. "Did Macalister come to see her?"

"Nay."

"Then we did not offend him. If he took her, he means to marry her."

"And then kill her," Ceanna whispered. Tears were already forming in her eyes when Ginnion put an arm around his wife. "We do not know he has her."

"Did Laird Gunn come to see her?" Justin asked.

Both of Shaw's eyebrows shot up. "Do you not remember? He had fire in his eyes when you would not let him see her."

"Then that is where we must search first," said Justin.

"We?" asked Ginnion.

"Am I to just sit here and wait, while my daughter is being...?" With women in the room and especially women who loved his daughter as much as he, Justin made himself stop. He took a long drink from his goblet and turned his attention once more to Blanka. "Where does Macalister live?"

"On the path from here, one would go north and then east. Macalister lives at the edge of the forest."

"Father, you have not eaten," Leslie pointed out. "You are of no use to Paisley if you do not eat."

He nodded and picked up his spoon, but instead of eating, he used it as a pointer. "We leave tomorrow and we will take many warriors with us."

"And leave the village unprotected?" Shaw asked. "Such might be exactly what they hope."

Everyone waited while Justin took a bite, thought that over, finished chewing and swallowed. 'Who is witless enough to think he could take our land and our families without a fight?"

"I do not know," Shaw answered. "Still, the clans grow in numbers and feeding them becomes more difficult daily. We have very good land."

"We have very good warriors too, who would come back and slaughter them. Nay, that is not what we must worry about most. Just in case, I shall take only fifty of our best fighters with me."

"Thirty," Ginnion put in. "Thirty are enough to protect you as well as Paisley when you find her."

"Thirty, then."

Shaw frowned. "Will you still send the lasses to visit their clans?"

"Aye, send them tomorrow, but only those from the nearest clans. When they come back, send more," Justin answered. "We must leave no stone unturned. Shaw, I leave you in command."

Those were the words Shaw did not want to hear. Ordinarily, he would not have spoken up but this time he was determined. "Paisley is my niece and I choose to go with you this time. Leave Ginnion in command."

"I'll not have that," Ginnion protested. "She is my niece too."

"And mine," said Essen, the man who married Justin's youngest sister, Patches.

Justin did not expect Carley's second husband to protest. Before Moan suffered a broken leg that still caused him a great deal of daily pain, he was Justin's second in command. He might be incapable of fighting as well as he once did, but there was nothing wrong with Moan's mind and he was one of Justin's favorite advisors.

"I am honored," said Moan before Justin even said it.

Paisley searched the bedchamber for a weapon, any sort of weapon and found nothing. The other three bedchambers on the fourth floor of the castle offered none either. "Stupid, stupid lad," Paisley whispered. "He thinks he is safe and therefore leaves nothing to defend himself with should he be forced up the stairs."

Of course, it was possible he removed them just before she arrived. In that case, she suspected he had them somewhere on the third floor. As quietly as she could, she went to the top of the stairs and peeked just far enough around the corner to see down. A guard stood at the bottom and as soon as he looked up, she jutted her head back and held her breath. Certain she was caught, she listened but she heard no footsteps on the stairs and at length, went back to her bedchamber. Seeing what was on the third floor was clearly out of the question.

Paisley went to the window again, although she kept her scarf on so she would not upset Macalister any more than necessary. As her courage once more increased, she went back across the hall to look down and see if perhaps that side of the castle was not so high up. It was the same four floors with no soft straw on the ground to fall on, if she decided to jump.

Another thought occurred to her and once more she went looking, only this time for rope. She could not imagine why anyone would have rope in a bedchamber, but she had come across odder things including kilts belonging to other clans.

With no success and no new ideas, there was nothing to do but sit on the bed and wait. Wait for what, she wondered. Marriage and death, she supposed. She could never let Rona die to save her from a dreadful marriage and would indeed agree to marry him if she could not escape it. What, she wondered, must a woman do to incite the kind of rage that caused Macalister to kill her *and* her daughters? Perhaps he simply hated women…and Paisley happened to be one.

Her thoughts were not helping and when Rona came back, she was glad for the company. This time she decided to play along. "Clean clothing? Thank you, Rona."

Rona carried them to the table and laid a white shirt, a folded plaid that matched her own and a new belt over the back of a chair. "You will wear them? He said you might refuse."

Paisley sighed. "I might as well get on with it." She began to untie her belt but then remembered the door was open. She went to it, peeked out and looked both ways before she closed it and went back to Rona.

"You have remembered?"

"Some, perhaps."

Rona came closer to look at her bruised chin again. The blue had deepened to black and both sides of her jaw were swollen. "Such a dreadful fall from your horse." She examined it closer still and wrinkled her brow. "I have never known anyone to land on their chin."

Paisley was glad the woman hadn't tried to touch her bruise. "That part I do not remember." As soon as her belt was loosened, her pleated MacGreagor plaid fell to the floor. "I had hoped to bathe before I dressed. Have you no loch nearby?"

"Aye, but it is very cold."

"On a hot summer day I would find it refreshing."

"The lads would have to go to protect you, and Laird Macalister would never allow the lads to see you unclothed."

"You mean he does not trust them to turn their backs?"

Rona leaned down, picked up the MacGreagor plaid and began to fold it. "Some he does, others not and with just cause. Before she died, his wife liked letting the lads look."

Paisley's eyes widened. "Oh, I see." She almost asked if his daughters liked to as well, but it was best to pretend she did not know about his past. "How did his wife die?"

"He killed her."

Rona said it so matter-of-factly it shocked Paisley. "He…"

"He did not mean to kill her, he meant only to punish her but hit her too hard." Rona took the green MacGreagor shirt from Paisley and helped her put on the clean white one. Then she handed the new belt to her mistress and was pleased when Paisley smiled.

"'Tis very fine workmanship," Paisley said, taking a moment to study the pattern in the leather. Smiling was painful, but she hoped to make Rona a trusting friend and knew no other way to accomplish it.

"'Twas his wife's belt. Laird Macalister had it made in particular."

Paisley balked and picked her own belt back up. "Then I must not wear it. Besides, my brother made this belt for me." She saw the worry in Rona's eyes and thought better of her decision. It was just a belt, after all. "On the other hand, this belt is much finer and if pleases him…"

"Aye, it will please him greatly, mistress."

Paisley put her belt back down on the table, wrapped the other around her waist and began to tie it. "Is the wee laddie his only child?"

"Save for three daughters. Once he learned of his wife's deceit, he sent them to the monastery to save their souls."

Paisley hid her surprise. "He must be a very good lad, then." Rona didn't reply as someone who agreed might have and Paisley noticed. Perhaps there was a smidgen of hope that Rona didn't like her laird as well as she pretended. Paisley decided to change the subject. "Tell me, how big is this clan?"

"We are small, but we are growing."

"How small, a hundred, two?"

"Two, perhaps."

"That is a very nice size and 'twill be easier for me to learn their names that way. We have nearly six hundred, very large and very strong warriors." She noticed Rona's eyes widen, but turned her attention to pleating the front of the Macalister plaid. "How long have you been servant here?"

"I am not a servant, I am his sister-in-law."

"I see, then his wife was your sister?"

"Aye."

They were both quiet for a time until she was finally dressed. Rona urged her to sit down, pulled a brush out of her own belt and removed Paisley's scarf. It reminded Paisley of how Leslie used to brush her hair and suddenly she was homesick beyond measure. "I have a sister too and four brothers. We are MacGreagors, have you heard of us?" She thought she felt Rona's hands tremble, but just for a moment.

"Aye, they are fierce warriors."

"Indeed they are, yet no finer lads ever lived. In our clan, if a lad hurts a lass out of anger he is put to death."

"I have heard that too. The other clans think it very odd."

"It has always been so and I find comfort in it. A wife should not have to fear her husband or any other lad. My very own father would do the killing."

Rona abruptly stopped brushing and stepped back to see the truth in Paisley's eyes. "You are Laird MacGreagor's daughter?" When Paisley nodded, Rona closed her eyes and crossed herself. She quickly glanced at the door and then leaned close enough to whisper, "He listens."

Paisley nodded her understanding. "'Tis enough brushing for now." She quickly stood up, wrapped her arms around Rona and whispered in her ear. "He said he would kill you if I deny him." She felt the woman stiffen and held on until she relaxed a little. When she let go, Paisley was smiling. "Might I have something more to eat? I find I am hungry now that the cool of the evening is certain to be upon us soon."

Rona was far from smiling, but she answered anyway. "I shall see to it directly."

*

If such a thing had to happen to Paisley, Justin was glad it was in the summer when the night sky was bright enough to allow time to prepare for the next day's ride. Nevertheless, all men needed rest and Justin was no exception. Before she went up to bed, Justin remembered to thank Blanka and assign a man to stay with her at all times while he was away. What the MacGreagors did not need was for yet another daughter to be carried off, especially Laird Monro's daughter. The man he chose to walk with her and turn his back while she bathed was Thomas, one of MacGreagors finest hunters.

It took time to settle down in his bed and relax, but his exhausted body demanded it and soon Justin was sound asleep.

*

Laird Chisholm Graham was beside himself with worry. As hard as he tried, he could not decide what to do or where to look for Paisley. Waiting for word of her was maddening and the thought of another man touching her made him grit his teeth, so he tried not to think about that. The market goods and tables were put away by the time he finally left his favorite seat on the trunk and went inside.

*

Tired and bored, Paisley let the cloth down over the window to darken the room and went to bed early, yet she kept her scarf on in case a noise drew her to the window. Her jaw still hurt and she did not like Macalister's wine well enough to use it to take away the pain. Chewing was far too painful, but for her evening meal, Rona brought porridge with milk and honey. The oats tasted good, needed little chewing and satisfied her hunger.

Even in her sleep, she heard every creak and groan of the aging castle, and hours later when she heard the bar being slowly lifted out of the lock on her door, she sat straight up. Terrified, she hurried out of bed and raced to the far end of the room.

First, someone slowly eased the door open and then a candle appeared, but the face behind the candle was not Laird Macalister's; it was Rona's. Paisley put her hand over her heart and took a forgotten breath.

Rona set the candle down on the table and untied a dagger sheath from around her own waist. She reached around Paisley, brought the strings to the front and tied them. "You must make good your escape," she whispered.

"He will kill you."

"Nay, he will not. I plied the guards with strong drink and they are asleep."

"Where do I go?"

"At the bottom of the stairs, turn to your left and go across the great hall. There is a small door in the back. Open it quietly, but first blow out the candle. 'Tis light enough still for you to see outside. Follow the path and it will take you into the forest."

Paisley kissed her new friend on the cheek. "I shall not forget you. If he dare lay a hand on you, my father will kill him. He may anyway when he hears who took me."

Rona smiled, "I am counting on that." She watched Paisley pick up the candle, slip out the door and disappear.

*

Sound asleep, Chisholm's eyes suddenly opened. He glanced around the room but no one was there and nothing seemed amiss. Still, he hesitated to close his eyes again. He felt oddly frightened, and then he remembered Paisley was missing, she needed him and he was not there. It was an overwhelming feeling of regret that refused to go away.

*

Paisley found it terrifying and tedious stepping over the legs of the sleeping guard on the stairs while praying the next wooden slat on the stairs would not creak as loudly as the last. On the second set of stairs, she could only avoid stepping on a man by putting her feet between his legs, but the board she put her weight on seemed to cry out in torture. Paisley held her breath, quickly stepped over his other leg and continued on. Behind her, the man changed positions, but he did not wake up.

At last, she managed to descend the final staircase without getting caught and turned into the great hall. The dying embers of a fire in this room afforded her enough light, so she blew out the candle and set it on the floor. Then she saw him.

*

On the fourth floor of the castle, Rona narrowed her eyes. All afternoon she questioned Macalister's warriors until one finally told her the truth -- her sister was brutally murdered and her nieces were not sent to a monastery, they were dead. A fierce anger boiled inside her and she began to consider a plot against him but first she wanted to make certain Paisley got away. With the aid of a little sleeping potion in the wine she served, Rona was certain the guards would not awake. She also let the old man in on her plan so he would not cry out and so far, everything was going just as she hoped.

Extremely cautious not to make a sound, Rona walked out the bedchamber door and then across the hall to the window in the opposite bedchamber. Directly beneath this room was Macalister's bedchamber and he never slept soundly enough for her comfort. By the time she served him the wine laced with sleeping aid, he said he'd had enough for one night and did not drink it. Therefore, if anyone prevented the escape, it would be Macalister himself and she dreaded what would become of them all if that happened.

*

In the scant light, a man started toward Paisley from the other end of the long room and as he walked, he oddly felt for and touched pieces of furniture. He is blind, Paisley realized. She was mindful not to breathe heavily as she eased away from the stairs toward a far wall, then she paused to see if the old man noticed.

If he knew she was there, he made no indication and it emboldened her. She took three steps toward the back door and was about to increase her speed when the old man abruptly stopped.

Paisley stopped too. She watched as the old man sniffed the air. He turned and seemed to be counting the steps to the hearth where the embers still glowed. It was unusual for anyone to light a fire on a hot day for warmth, but perhaps the old man got cold in the evenings like she did.

After he counted five paces, he knelt down and began to feel the floor for hot spots. "He'll burn us all alive someday," the old man muttered.

She seized the opportunity and as quietly as she could, headed for the back door. Step after step brought her closer to freedom and she was tempted to run, but the old man could still cry out and give her away. When she reached the door, she remembered to open it slowly just as Rona said and when it was wide enough, she slid through and stepped out onto the path. Just as slowly, she closed the door behind her.

Cautiously she began to walk up the path, trying to look calm should anyone see her, but no one tended the smoldering campfires along the way, none stood in cottage doorways and there were no guards to catch her.

At last, Paisley walked into the forest and disappeared.

CHAPTER V

It seemed like hours before Rona finally spotted Paisley walking past the embers of a small outside fire. Rona turned from the window and grinned. Soon the sun would come up and her day would begin. This day would be Rona's day and her revenge would be sweet indeed.

*

In the dim night light, the edge of the forest was not so difficult to navigate. She moved the tall leaves of the ferns aside, skirted around shrubs too high to step over and kept going straight ahead. Yet when she entered the deeper parts of the forest, where huge Douglas Fir and Scots Pine grew, the night became steadily darker.

She was glad her new shoes fit well, tried not to walk into a tree and feared she was getting lost. Not knowing how long she slept, she had no concept of time and could only hope the sun would soon be rising. No amount of wishing helped as she walked around trees and stepped between or over bush after bush. Only when she looked straight up could she see the scant light of the sky.

Becoming anxious, Paisley began to suspect something or someone was watching her. Were they the eyes of a gray wolf, an elk, a wild boar or worse -- Laird Macalister? Just in case, she drew her dagger and prepared herself to lash out no matter the attacker. She moved on, looking from side to side often, calculating the best place to stab a man or an animal and hoping her foreboding was only in her mind.

She walked until she could walk no more.

Her feet hurt, her plaid kept catching on the bushes and she had no idea where she was. The forest was nearly pitch black causing her to stumble and nearly fall twice. At last, she found a small clearing, sat down, put her back against a tree trunk and rested. Yet she was afraid to fall asleep and kept her dagger clutched in her hand. She looked for eyes watching her but saw nothing. Nevertheless, she could not shake the foreboding and kept alert to any and all movement.

At least nothing could grab her from behind with her back to the tree. She trembled at the memory of the man grabbing her and wondered if she would ever get over it. It was the most frightening thing that had ever happened to her.

For a time she wondered if Chisholm was looking for her as she knew her father must be. Still, how would he know where to look…how would any of them know where to look? It was comforting to think Chisholm might be searching for her. Perhaps he would be around the next tree or… No, her mind was running away with her and she needed to concentrate on the problem at hand -- the eyes in the forest.

Paisley couldn't seem to keep from trembling and knew not if she was cold or just frightened out of her wits. She was also tired and yawned twice, but she charged herself not to sleep, not yet and certainly not there.

*

By the time the rooster crowed, Justin was already up and getting dressed. As soon as he finished, he walked to his window, drew back the covering and looked out. Thirty of his men were gathered in the glen loading pack horses with supplies. So also were four women with husbands and two more men preparing to go to the nearest clans. He was pleased.

Justin hurried down the first flight of stairs, opened the door to the bedchamber his oldest sons shared and found it empty. Equally pleased, he rushed down the last flight of stairs, found all four of his sons and a morning meal waiting for him. All of his sisters were there too, but it was to his daughter, Leslie, he went first. He hugged her and tried to calm the fear in her eyes. "We will find her, I promise."

Leslie nodded and watched him hug each of his sisters as he always did before going on a journey. Next, he examined Sawney's neck. The wound was healing well and it was one less thing to worry about. He mussed the hair of his other sons and sat down. Abruptly, he stood back up. "Blanka, do sit and eat."

She did as he said and noticed he waited for the other women to sit before he retook his chair. It was an odd custom, one she had never seen before, but she said nothing.

*

Chisholm's morning meal was over and with nothing better to do but wait for news, he decided to go for a walk to ease his tense and stiff muscles. Sleep had not been kind to him and when he could finally go back to sleep, he spent most of the night tossing and turning. Long ago, he rejected the idea that he needed a guard to constantly protect him in a place where people wanted him to keep providing clans with wares. He was a fair and reasonable man, word had it, and as long as he remained so, he was in little danger of being attacked or called out.

He headed toward the meadow to take his walk and hadn't gone far before he abruptly stopped. Before him lay the two MacDuff brothers with their beloved deerhound stretched out on his back, sound asleep between them. With his right paw, the dog swished the air ridding himself of a pesky fly and Chisholm couldn't help but smile. Ross lay on his side in a fetal position and had an arm over his eyes to shield himself from the light while his brother, Adair, lay flat on his back loudly snoring. Each had scruffy beards, long blond hair that had not been washed and frayed shirts and kilts. Neither bothered to take off his weapons before he slept, which was always a good idea. Chisholm admired Adair's sword the most. It was clearly bent outward about a quarter of the way from the tip. No matter, these two were more likely to run than fight.

The followers of Laird MacDuff were not known for working the land or making things. In fact, they were not known for anything save a swift surrender when threatened. The laird who chose to capture that clan would soon regret it, for the MacDuffs were an unpredictable lot.

Chisholm knew these two brothers well and it was not unusual to find them sleeping somewhere nearby. They seldom bartered for goods, but they liked to hear the gossip and watch the women. Apparently, he guessed, they had nothing better to do and no one in the MacDuff clan cared where they were.

The overly friendly dog awoke, spotted Chisholm, wiggled until it could get to its feet and walked over Ross to excitedly greet Chisholm. Ross woke up with a start, reached over and shook his brother.

"What?" At the sight of Laird Graham, Adair's eyes widened and he quickly scooted away.

Both brothers looked uncommonly alarmed and Chisholm found it very odd. "Have I frightened you?"

"Nay," Adair answered a little too quickly.

"We are late," Ross said. He hurried to get up and leaned down to pick up the spare MacDuff plaid he used for a blanket.

"Late for what?" asked Chisholm. The overly friendly and very large dog demanded his attention and tried to jump up on him. Chisholm loved dogs and this one was a particular beauty. As did most deerhounds, the dog had a long reddish-brown coat and mane, a white chest, a straggly white beard and a long, upward curved tail with hair that nearly touched the ground. His dark eyes betrayed his eagerness to please and when, after a good rubbing Chisholm told him to sit, the dog obeyed.

The brothers exchanged worried glances. "You did not frighten us," said Adair.

"I believe we got beyond that question. For what are you late?" The brothers hesitated, exchanged glances again and Chisholm became even more suspicious. "You are up to something, I see."

Confused, Ross wrinkled his brow. "See what?"

"That you have stolen something you do not want me to discover. What is it?"

Both widened their eyes. "We are not thieves," said Ross. He let his chest swell just a little. "MacDuffs do not steal."

"Then it is something else. Perhaps you have heard something about Paisley MacGreagor. Do you know who has taken her?"

Adair bent down to scratch his lower leg. "Well, we..." All of a sudden, he felt Ross kick his backside and soon, he was flat on his face in the meadow. "Why did you do that?" he shouted, turning over and then quickly getting back up.

"You promised not to tell," Ross yelled.

"I was not going to tell, witless."

"Who is witless, me or him?"

Adair rolled his eyes. "You...witless."

The sun rising in the southeast made the jewels in Chisholm's necklace sparkle and Ross would have liked touching them once more, but instead he pulled his brother backward. As soon as he decided they were far enough away, he yelled, "Run!"

Both brothers spun around and ran for their horses with the deerhound close behind.

They knew something, Chisholm was sure of it. Fortunately, the people were already setting up the tables and adding an array of food. Shouting for his horse to be brought around with all due haste, he ran to a table, grabbed a cloth sack, filled it with bread, apples and cheese and quickly drew the strings. He tied the sack around his waist and ran toward the stables. The brothers were already out of sight, but with any luck at all he would soon catch up to them.

*

Finally, the sky had begun to brighten and she could better see where she was going. Feeling a little better after resting a minute or two, she lifted her skirt to examine the scratches on her ankles and lower legs. She had no choice other than to raise her skirt as she walked and her scratches were the price she paid. No wild animals got to her in the night and neither did Laird Macalister. For that, she was very thankful. Now it was thirst that plagued her.

Paisley closed her eyes and tried to listen for the sound of water, but if a creek was nearby, she could not hear it. The forest was never completely quiet. There were always rustling leaves, small animals moving the bushes and chirping birds in the trees, but at least she did not hear someone following her.

She was worried about Rona and tried not to imagine Laird Macalister hurting her. What story could Rona tell a man like Macalister to keep him from suspecting? She should not have escaped, she should have stayed for Rona's sake, but she did not think about that at the time. All she thought about was being free. Now, she was free, thirsty, cold and completely lost.

Her uncle's training taught her to know where the sun was and go back the way she came if she got lost. It was little help to her now. Although she was sure the sun was rising in the east, she was knocked out and had no idea which way her abductor took her. Did he go east to the edge of the forest, west, south or perhaps north? Paisley did not even know where the edge of the forest was in any direction from the MacGreagor glen. She knew there were oceans both east and west, but that knowledge was equally useless.

She tried to remember what else Ginnion taught her. All clans had a water source of some kind, therefore, all she needed to do was find a creek and follow it downhill. However, he neglected to teach her exactly how to find a creek. Her horse could find one -- if she had a horse.

*

The one Rona planned for her brother-in-law, laird over all the

Macalisters, would not be an easy death. Every morning Macalister complained of an upset stomach, no doubt from drinking his bitter wine, and Rona religiously mixed a potion with still more wine to ease his discomfort.

There was much Macalister did not know about Rona.

Assured she believed his lies, he trusted her more than anyone else to care for him and when he found his morning drink already prepared, he was not surprised. It was a pity, he often thought, she was not as becoming as her sister, for she seemed to love him. She never interfered, always wished to please him and in return, he favored her with an occasional smile. He designated most of his ordinary and otherwise mundane chores to his second in command so he could concentrate on planning his entire life in abundant detail. Therefore, when he sat down at the table in the great hall that morning, no one was there save the old, blind man.

The great hall in the castle was plain and ordinary compared to the room Paisley was kept in and for a very good reason -- in his rage, Macalister destroyed some of the finer furnishings. A wine stain from a thrown goblet could not be removed from a painting without the paint being disturbed and therefore it was burned and the wall left bare. A Viking ax yanked off the wall had been used to completely destroy a matching set of small oak tables brought from London, window coverings were yanked down, chairs were smashed against the stonewalls and his fury did not end for nearly an hour.

When he calmed, he made Rona clean up the mess and simply sent a man off to secure more fine furnishings from London. Unfortunately, the new items did not arrive before his bride, but they would before the wedding and he greatly anticipated the arrival. He did not suspect the man he sent made off with the gold and silver coins, never to be seen again.

One important thing he did not know about Rona was her interest in poisons. She often spent her free time with the soothsayers, growing plants and learning which leaf or berry did what. It was to help her laird in case of invasion, she convinced herself, then and only then would she use it.

Today she would make an exception. In the kitchen of Macalister's castle, she made his usual porridge, added a touch of liquid from the Nightshade stem and a smidgeon of finely crushed Foxglove flowers. A generous helping of honey, she hoped, would sufficiently cover any bitter taste.

Rona smiled. All along she felt something was amiss, but he always had the perfect answer to every question. She understood why he killed his wife and if he knew the whole truth, she'd not have lived as long as she did. The son and daughters he called his, could have been fathered by any number of men. Still, they were her loved ones and killing her nieces was the unforgivable deed. It was cruel, even for him and he could never explain it away with his lies, no matter what he said.

Once her sister and nieces were gone from the castle, Rona was all the little boy had and it was for him she stayed. Not wanting him to see, she took the child to a cottage to play with another his age before she began preparing the morning meal. Soon the child would be fatherless too, but not quite yet. First, Macalister would suffer.

Nursing his morning tonic, Macalister rarely had anything to say to the old man who sat at the other end of the table. Many times after he murdered his wife, he threw the old man out only to find him there again the next morning. It was to make him suffer for what he did, Macalister believed, but he felt no remorse. Giving up finally, he learned to simply tolerate the old man, although it did slightly annoy him still. Macalister watched Rona set the food in front of him. "I desire to eat with my bride this morning."

"You cannot."

He narrowed his eyes, but she expected it. "She is in the womanly way."

Macalister quickly lowered his gaze. "Oh, I see." It meant his plans for a speedy marriage would have to wait another week or so. "Have you fed her?"

"Aye and I gave her a tonic for her pain. She is asleep, I believe."

"Take good care of her, I promised she would not suffer."

Rona nodded, set another bowl down in front of the blind man, guided his hand to the edge of it, and then started up the stairs. As she went up, one of the guards came down, holding his throbbing head. "I pray you slept well," she said.

He only grunted and once he was gone, she smiled. She climbed the last two staircases expecting to see more guards, but they must have left while she was in the kitchen. Her plan was working perfectly. When she reached the fourth floor and walked into the room Paisley had been kept in, she sat down at the small table and began to eat the meal she pretended to make for his captive bride.

The food was cold, but she had eaten worse. Macalister was not a patient man with people or food and was prone to quickly consume an entire meal. Therefore, Rona was not surprised when she heard his faint cry three floors down. First, his heart would begin to race, she knew, and then the leaves of the Nightshade would begin to paralyze him.

Even when Macalister began to shout, she continued eating her meal as if she had not a care in the world. Then she heard the huge front door creak open and slam shut, rushed out of the room and hurried down the stairs.

Rona found Macalister just as she expected. He was slumping on the table about to fall off with his eyelids drooping. At the other end of the table near the old man stood his second and third in command with their mouths open. They did not attempt to help their laird and that too she expected, for neither cared if he fell off the table or not. They were both good men, hated Macalister and she did not fear either of them.

"Have you done this, Rona?" one asked.

She knew Macalister could hear every word, but just in case, she moved closer to him. "He should not have lied to me." Although his lids drooped, she saw a slight flicker in his eyes and it greatly pleased her.

"Rona, the king will have you executed for this."

"'Twill be an honorable death," said she.

The second in command grabbed the other man's arm. "The king will never hear it from us. Let him die in bed with no mark on him."

"Aye," said the first. "And let us live in peace."

"Is he dead?" asked the old man.

Rona grinned, "Nay, I wanted him to know who betrayed him, but a little more poison should do him in." She saw Macalister struggle to move. "Fear me, do you? 'Tis about time." She grabbed his bowl and headed for the kitchen to make one more bite of porridge. This time, she added plenty of poison.

By the time she went back into the great hall, the men were dragging Macalister up to his third floor bedchamber. Thrilled with her freedom, she set the bowl on the table, threw back the dreadful window coverings and let in the fresh air and sunshine. Macalister had plenty of excuses to keep it dark, but she suspected it was to keep him from seeing what he had done to his own father. The old man was hardly guilty of anything, but he happened upon Macalister's wife when she was undressed and for that, he was severely punished.

"Tis a great day," she muttered, touching the old man on the shoulder as she picked the bowl back up.

"Aye," was all he said.

CHAPTER VI

It wasn't that hard to catch up with the MacDuff brothers after all. They kept to the well-worn path traveling east and their dog raced back to Chisholm often. Each time he got down off his horse, gave the dog a much deserved scratching behind the ears or under his chin to encourage him and then watched him run off again. For a time, Chisholm wondered if the brothers truly knew where Paisley was. Still, this was his only lead and at least now, he was doing something other than just sitting on the trunk waiting for gossip.

At the junction of the paths, Chisholm halted his horse. The one to his left would take them to the river, the MacGreagors and the MacDuffs, while the one straight ahead led to other clans. Which did they take? He looked for fresh tracks in the dirt but there were several, and it was not until the dog came racing back that he knew the brothers had continued east. He found it comforting to know they were not headed home.

Twice more the dog came back to be petted and twice more he ran off after the brothers. By the time the sun was high in the sky, Chisholm wondered if the brothers were wise enough to let their horses rest, but he began to hear voices and recognized them. He halted his horse, dismounted and tied the reins to a tree. The dog, he knew, would probably give him away, but he was willing to chance it just so he could hear better. He crept forward until he could stand behind two trees and see every move they made.

Ross dumped water out of his flask and began to refill it in a creek. "She is probably already dead."

"Then she'll not likely marry me," said Adair.

"She would not likely marry you alive or dead."

"Why not, I am the handsome one."

"Aye, but I am stronger and many a lass prefers the strong lads."

Adair finished filling his flask and pushed the stopper back in place. "I am younger. I will be as strong as you once I am grown. Then I will be handsome and strong."

Ross rolled his eyes. "She will prefer me." He dug half a loaf of bread out of his sack, sat down and took a big bite.

Behind a bush, Chisholm was tempted to force them to tell him where Paisley was, but he couldn't be certain she was the woman they were talking about.

"Father said we best not take a wife until we build another cottage. We cannot both stay under the same room with her, now can we?" said Adair. "The cottage is mine; therefore it is you who must build another."

Ross broke what remained of his bread in half and handed it to his brother. "Me? I do not know how to build a cottage."

"Aye, but you are the strong one, remember?"

Just then, the dog appeared, leapt into Adair's lap and nearly knocked him over. "There you are, Mutton." He strained against the weight of the dog and plopped the last bite of bread in his mouth before the dog could get it.

"Mutton," Ross snickered. "Mutton is sheep, not dog, everyone knows that."

"Aye, but the dog likes to chase sheep. Mutton chases mutton, do you see?"

Chisholm had to restrain himself to keep from laughing. He didn't do it well enough and soon the dog stood next to him, wildly wagging its tail demanding attention. He quickly knelt down to pet him and looked back, but the brothers did not seem to care where the dog was.

"The thing is," Adair was saying, "how do we get her out."

"The place is clearly haunted," said Ross.

"Aye, by an old blind lad what caught us."

"And yelled for help. 'Tis your fault, you did not watch where you were going and ran right into him."

"'Twas dark, remember?" Adair shot back. "I nearly broke a leg. At least 'twas me who thought to tell the laird about the bonnie lass so he would let us go. I saved us."

"Well I'm not going back in that castle. 'Tis dark, 'tis haunted and it smells."

"Not even to make Paisley MacGreagor your bride?"

At last they said her name and Chisholm wondered why he had not thought of that before. Of course Macalister took her, he was a greedy man who wanted only the best of everything and a fetching wife would be high on his list. Chisholm abruptly stood up and stepped out from behind the bush. "I will get her out and you will help me."

The brothers could not have been more shocked. Both instantly got to their feet and backed away until Ross almost fell over a bush. Then Adair mustered some measure of courage. "What will you give us to help you?"

"Brother!" Ross said, shoving his brother away. "You cannot make demands."

"Did I not say four cows and one bull? 'Tis yours when we bring her home," answered Chisholm.

Adair regained his balance and suspiciously glared at Chisholm. "You want her for yourself, am I right?"

"I do, but I too must win her. You are the handsome one, he is the strong one and I am only a laird. I say we see which she will choose." Both brothers nodded. It seemed being a laird did not impress the MacDuff brothers much and for a moment, Chisholm wondered if Paisley might think the same. After all, she was the daughter of a laird and knew all the disadvantages. He decided to worry about that later.

They waited for the horses to rest while Chisholm ate his noon meal and played with the rambunctious dog. He tossed a stick away and the dog was more than happy to retrieve it repeatedly. "Tell me why you went inside Macalister's castle." It was apparently the wrong question to ask. The brothers glared at each other as if to dare one to answer.

"Well then," Chisholm tried again, "How did you breach the castle? Were the doors not bolted?"

"Not the small one in the back," said Adair, "and as we are small lads."

"We are not small," Ross argued.

"Small enough to go through the door. I should like to see a MacGreagor fit it," said Adair.

About that Ross had no argument.

"Was it at night that you entered?" asked Chisholm.

Ross rolled his eyes, "Not until we got inside, the covers were all let down on the windows."

"We were hungry and…" Adair began.

"You hoped to steal food, then?" asked Chisholm.

Adair grinned. "A laird can afford it, we steal from…" Once more, Ross shoved his brother.

"From me? Ah, so that is why my honey bread disappears. In the future, you may ask when you are hungry. The Graham will not deny you."

"I told you to ask," Ross sneered.

"You did not, when?"

Chisholm was getting nowhere fast with this conversation. "Did you know Laird Macalister killed his wife and daughters?"

"Aye, 'twas why we greatly feared him when he caught us," Adair answered. "But we could not know he would take Paisley, we swear it."

"I believe you."

Ross snickered. "He took her right out from under Laird MacGreagor's nose. Macalister is daft."

"Aye," agreed Adair, "Mean *and* daft!"

They talked for a while longer but Chisholm was eager to get going. He decided the horses had rested long enough, the three of them mounted and started for the land of the Macalister.

*

Paisley awoke with a start. She must have fallen asleep and her first instinct was to look around for any kind of danger. Satisfied she was alone, she relaxed a little and got up. It was daytime, she could finally see much better and the birds chirping in the trees comforted her. It was then that she smelled smoke. At first she feared a forest fire but it had been days since rain, lightning or thunder graced the land of Scotland. It was another smell that made her sniff the air -- the smell of hot cakes. Where there were hot cakes, there were men and where there were men, there was water. She brushed off the back of her plaid and began to creep toward the odor.

Not but a few yards away, three men sat around a small fire making their noon meal. She hid behind a tree, peeked out and licked her lips.

"Are you hungry, lass?"

The voice of a man behind her made her jump nearly out of her skin. The man took hold of her by the arm and pulled her out into the open. "Macalister sends a lass to spy on us."

The other three laughed. "Aye, and a bonny lass at that," said one.

"I'll have her for my own," said another. "I have want of a wife."

"I am already married," Paisley scoffed. The lie hadn't worked on Macalister, but it might work on them. "And I am not a spy, I am lost."

The man holding her arm forced her to sit on the ground before he let go of her. "No doubt Macalister told her to claim that if she got caught."

"I am not a Macalister," she demanded. "I am Paisley, second daughter of Laird Justin MacGreagor."

Again the men laughed. "A MacGreagor who wears the colors of the Macalisters?" a man teased. "Does your husband know?"

Paisley closed her eyes and hung her head.

Blathan was Laird Keith's second in command, sat closest to her and was beginning to take pity. He didn't believe a word she said, but any woman in Macalister's clan deserved pity.

When she lifted her eyes, Blathan's smile seemed the most kind. He was a well-proportioned man for his height, with red hair and green eyes. "I thirst."

He untied his flask, pulled out the stopper and once he noticed the bruise under her chin, he helped her hold it to her mouth while she drank. When she finished, he tied the flask back around his waist. "Who hit you?"

She answered before she realized how it would sound, "A Macalister." Again they laughed at her.

"What did you do to deserve it, lass?" one asked.

"I have done nothing wrong and I am not a Macalister," she demanded through gritted teeth, although it soon caused her considerable pain.

"If not a spy, what then?" asked Blathan.

"As I said, I am lost."

"How did you get lost?"

"In this forest it is quite easy, I have discovered."

"That much is true." Blathan picked up his bowl and let her have the last of his hot cake. He watched her gobble it down and for a moment, he almost believed her. But then, if she was a Macalister spy, he could hardly let her go. "You shall go with us," he said at last.

She studied his eyes for a moment. He seemed harmless enough and she still had a dagger in case she needed it. "Do you not want to hear how I came to be lost?"

"Nay!"

That, she did not understand at all. The Scots were a curious people and why not let her tell them? "To where do you go?"

"Home, we shall let our laird say what to do with you." Blathan got up. "We shall hear no more of your lies." The meal was over and it would be a while yet before he would see his wife and children. Before one of his unmarried men could claim Paisley, he announced she would ride with him. Claiming a woman was the same as betrothing her. There was just a slight possibility she was who she said she was and if so, he wanted no part of a war with the MacGreagors. A man who claimed a woman does not often want to give her back, even to a fearsome father like Justin MacGreagor.

As soon as their things were gathered and the fire put out, Blathan mounted his horse, gave her his arm and helped her swing up behind him.

It felt good to ride instead of walk. She did not completely trust these strangers, all of which had red hair and looked as if they were brothers, but if they truly took her to their laird, perhaps he would hear her story and see that she got home safely. Not only that, there would be women to help her bathe and get out of the hateful Macalister colors. Paisley was willing to wear most anything not to smell like Macalister's castle any longer.

*

Just as he had when he entered the Kennedy hold, Justin and his thirty men rode directly through the center of the Gunn village to the courtyard in front of the Keep. Just as it had been in the Kennedy village, the thunder of so many horses made Laird Gunn burst out of his door to see what was at hand. He was very old, no longer a brave man and as soon as he saw the size of the invaders, he was ready to surrender.

Laird Gunn's eyes bulged as he watched Justin swing down off his horse and draw his sword. From the door of several cottages, men and women rushed out and when the Gunns drew their swords, so did the MacGreagors.

"Stowe your weapons, lads," Shaw shouted. "We are not here to fight unless we must." Both sides felt relieved, except Laird Gunn who openly shook at the sight of the much taller man holding a sword not two inches from his chest.

"I have come for my daughter." Justin was not as enraged as before but he was just as determined.

"Who is your daughter?"

"Paisley MacGreagor."

"The one with white hair? She is *your* daughter?"

"The same, give her back and she best not be harmed."

Laird Gunn glanced down the row of MacGreagor warriors and briefly wondered where he might find such men. "If I had her, I would surely give her back. 'Tis true, some of my lads need wives, but we do not so boldly take them and not one with white hair easily recognized. A man who did that would have to be daft...unless."

"Unless what?"

"I have heard, if a lass boils the fall leaves of yellow and red, she can change her golden hair to red. I have never seen it done, but..."

Justin stopped listening. There was an old fable in his clan, but he had not told that story in years. Still, the boiling of leaves truly can change the color of hair. If the color of her hair had changed, it would be far more difficult for anyone to find her. Justin put his sword away. "Do you know who took her?"

His opponent was calming down and so was Laird Gunn. "I can think of no one save Laird Macalister. We heard tell he was searching the land to find the most comely lass in Scotland. If he has her, he will not kill her, he will marry her." He paused to take a deep breath. "Will you kill him?"

"Would you care if I did?"

Realizing he just escaped death, Laird Gunn took another relieved breath. "Not at all. He is a blight on the land, cruel to his women and his animals alike. Do you truly offer a golden chalice?"

"I do."

"I should like to see it someday."

Justin was not quite certain why he believed Laird Gunn but he did. "After my daughter is home, I will send word for you to come. You will be welcome on our land." He nodded once more and mounted his horse.

*

It was afternoon when Justin turned his men and rode back out of the Gunn village. From Blanka's description, finding Macalister's castle would not be difficult and Justin intended to keep going, but Shaw convinced him to stop and rest in a meadow just off the path.

Sacks hung over the backs of the pack horses offered smoked meat, raw vegetables and plenty of bread for hungry warriors. Most preferred to stand in a wide circle instead of sitting while they ate and most tried to ignore their pacing laird.

Justin finally stopped and looked at his men. "Who here has seen Macalister's castle?"

"Did we not pass it when last we went to see the King?" Andrew asked.

Justin wrinkled his brow, "Is that the one? As I recall, no one lived there at the time."

"Aye, we wanted to see it up close, but you were eager to get home, as I recall."

"I wish now that I had stopped," Justin admitted. "'Tis an English castle, it is not?"

"Aye but the English run off years ago." Andrew walked a little closer to his laird. He was pleased to have something to offer none of the other men had. "My father spoke of seeing it once as a laddie. The plague killed most, the English blamed it on the Scots and those that lived fled back to England."

"I pray we never see another plague like that one." Justin said and noticed a couple of men crossing themselves. The worst of all plagues killed thousands and came before he was born, but his father spoke of it often. It killed with such speed the clan hardly had time to make boxes for the burials. More often than not, children were put in the same box as parents to save time and wood.

"'Twas likely the English that gave the plague to the Scots," another man grumbled and the rest of them heartily agreed.

Any other time Justin would also have enjoyed the comment. Instead he asked, "How do we attack an English castle?"

For the better part of an hour they discussed the advantages and the disadvantages, until it was agreed they needed to see it before deciding. An end to the conversation was all it took for Justin to mount up and head through the forest to find the path that would take him to Macalister's land.

*

Thomas MacGreagor did not mind walking with Blanka Monro in the glen he called home. He was a hunter but hunting had been plentiful lately, the clan had enough meat for a while, and Blanka needed protection. All the warriors were far more alert than they had been before Paisley was taken and much discussion about the clan's vulnerability had already taken place. Usually a place where the women got their exercise and the children played, there were markedly more men in the glen. Even so, Thomas often watched the trees just to make sure he could not detect some sort of movement.

All his attention to protecting her made Blanka a little ill at ease. She appreciated it, and in fact was used to it, but for a second day she was in the home of strangers who most likely had better things to do. She felt a burden but there wasn't much she could do about it. Her father left her there and that was that.

"Are you unwell?" Thomas asked soon after they reached the middle of the glen.

The question surprised Blanka. "Do I look unwell?"

"Not at all. It is just that you keep wringing your hands and my mother does that when she is unwell."

Blanka quickly dropped her hands to her sides. The sun brought out the red in her brown hair and her fair complexion seemed in need of a little color. "If you must know, I am displeased."

Thomas instantly stopped walking and turned to her. "Do I

displease you?"

"You? Not at all, 'tis my father who displeases me. He left me here hoping Laird MacGreagor will take me for his wife."

"So I have heard. You do not prefer our laird? Many a lass in our clan does."

"I find nothing unsightly about him, if that is what you mean, but I would much rather not be a mistress."

"A lass who does not want to be a mistress? 'Tis unheard of."

She realized he was teasing her and returned his pleasant smile. His hair was nearly the same color as hers which he wore pulled back and tied. His beard was slightly lighter and his mustache was well trimmed. "As long as I can remember, I wanted to be queen, but alas, the king is…well, he is…"

"Already married?"

"That too," she said and started them walking again. Thomas was a far more pleasant man than she expected and she was beginning to like his company.

"What other is he?"

"He has a particular failing in his character."

"A failing?" Thomas quickly glanced around pretending to make sure no one else could hear and leaned a little closer, "The King of Scots is a bit odd, is he? I am shocked to hear it."

"I swear 'tis true, the king likes my father."

"Nay," Thomas scoffed.

She couldn't help but giggle. "I simply cannot forgive the King for it, do you blame me?"

"Well, I do not know your father, but if you say…" He quickly grabbed her arm and pulled her back before she stepped in a hole and twisted her ankle. She looked upset for a moment until he pointed down. " 'Tis where lightning_struck once. We fill it, but the rain washes the dirt away."

Blanka nodded and as soon as he let go of her arm, she walked around the hole to the corral to look at the stallions. A horse with a golden coat and a white mane instantly caught her eye.

"Do you like to ride?" he asked.

"I did before my father decided to marry me off. Now I dread the journey home when he returns. 'Tis a good week of riding, maybe more, and I am not at all fond of sleeping in the forest..." she started to giggle again.

"What?"

"I am not fond of sleeping in the forest with no less than fifty snoring lads nearby."

Thomas chuckled. "Tis the same for all Scots, I have heard. Do you suppose the English snore?"

"I doubt the King of England would allow it. If you believe the gossip, he is a stern lad who does not abide anything he does not personally command. Do you believe the English are as brutal as we have heard?"

"Aye they are, and we can be as fierce as they believe us to be. I pity the lad who took Paisley for he will surely die and perhaps many with him."

Blanka sighed. "Some lads deserve to die. They treat women as animals, sometimes worse, and my father turns a blind eye to it all."

"There will always be lads who harm lasses and children. We

occasionally have one or two in our numbers, but the punishment is swift and without mercy."

She glanced around at the other people in the glen. "Everyone seems to live in peace here."

"Today we live in peace but it cannot last. There are rumblings among us. Some lads desire more adventure than Justin allows and they wish for the power he has. The day may come when it is no longer possible to keep our lives the same."

"You speak as a lad who knows. Do you want to be the MacGreagor laird someday?"

"Not I, but there is one I fear will soon challenge our ways."

Blanka turned away from the horses in favor of watching the children play. The little ones tried to catch the older, who could easily outrun them and then turn to taunt their pursuer. Other boys, not yet old enough for formal training, challenged each other with wooden swords, while a warrior nearby made sure they didn't poke an eye out. Watching them made her smile and she easily changed the subject. "What is the most glorious thing you have ever seen?"

He started to say she was and that thought came as a total surprise to him. He enjoyed her company and she was pleasing to look at, but they had only just met the day before and there were limits to what a man could say to the daughter of a laird. "A golden eagle."

"For me it is a child's first smile. I can never get enough of seeing it and cannot wait until it is my own child who smiles at me."

"Then I hope you will have many smiles to choose from."

*

It had taken a long time for Laird Macalister to die which amazed

Rona. When he did not easily swallow the porridge, she tried poison in wine, in broth and even in water, but with his face void of muscles, it was hard to make him drink. Most spilled out of his mouth into the bowl she held under his chin. As a last resort, she spoon-fed him the liquid and held his mouth closed until it went down his throat. At last, he drew his final breath.

"'Tis a pity we carried him up only to carry him down again," said his second in command when it was over.

"Throw him out the window." Rona didn't smile and the men were not certain if she meant it. "Do you fear breaking his neck?"

Both men grinned, turned Laird Macalister's body sideways on the bed and then each took hold of an arm and a leg while Rona looked out the window to be sure Macalister would not land on anyone in the courtyard. With the coast clear, they carried him to the window and with a one, two, three, heaved the man out head first. Then they listened to the thud of his body hitting the dirt.

Rona finally smiled. "Clearly, it was the fall that killed him."

"I can think of no other explanation," Macalister's second in command said.

"Nor can I," said the third.

It had been such a pleasure watching those flickers of horror in Macalister's eyes as she fed him more poison, and she hoped someday she might feel some measure of regret. Not this day, however, this day she was thrilled.

How a deathly ill man managed to fall out the window of his second floor bedchamber was a secret between the three of them, and that particular bit of juicy gossip would not spread all over Scotland.

However, the sight of a man flying out of his own castle and falling to his death before the clan's very eyes surely would.

*

Three men on horseback hid behind trees at the edge of the forest and watched the man fly out a window. Then they watched the clan begin to slowly gather around the body in the castle courtyard.

For a change, the dog was behaving himself and sat down beside Chisholm's horse. That was before he spotted sheep in the meadow and what was a dog for if not to chase sheep? Abruptly, off he went, scrambling toward the meadow and the unsuspecting ewe.

"A fitting end for an unfit lad," said Ross, sitting on his swayback horse between Chisholm and Adair.

"Who?" asked Chisholm, keeping his voice down so they would not be discovered.

"Lest my eyes deceive me that be Laird Macalister."

Chisholm raised an eyebrow. "Truly?"

"Aye," Adair agreed. "She is safe now, at least from him."

Chisholm wrinkled his brow. "Are there more dangers you care to tell me about?"

Ross smirked. "She is in no danger from me; I choose not to marry her. A lad could spend a lifetime trying to find her each time she is snatched away."

"What other danger is she in?" Chisholm asked.

"Well, the two of you still want her and Macalister warriors will as well once they lay eyes on her." Ross sighed. "The one who claims her will soon regret it."

Adair nodded. "If my brother does no want her, then neither do I."

"So you have seen her?"

Instantly, both brothers caught their breaths. "Well, we…"

"How close to the MacGreagor glen did you get?"

"We only saw her from afar," Adair tried.

"But close enough to know she is a bonnie lass?"

Ross folded his arms. "We have heard rumors, the same as every other lad."

"Have the MacGreagors caught you?"

"Twice," Adair said. Then he quickly moved his horse out of reach so his brother could not shove him off.

Chisholm smiled, turned his attention back to the people still gathering around their laird's body and decided now, while the people were distracted, would be the best time to see to Paisley's safety. He urged his horse out of the trees onto the path that led to the courtyard in front of the large doors of the castle.

It was a foreboding building made of gray stone and mortar as others were, only with darker, more ominous stones. The windows on the first floor were not covered as the brother's had described, although, except for the one Macalister came flying out of, those on the other floors were. The double wooden doors were massive and no doubt bolted from the inside, which meant Chisholm would have to find a way to get someone to open them.

He was almost halfway to the courtyard when he glanced back and discovered the brothers were not with him. He halted his horse, turned it around and glared until the brothers shrugged and reluctantly came out of the trees. Once more he started down the path between cottages that were kept in good repair, no doubt to please the image

Macalister wished to portray. For a moment, Chisholm hoped Paisley was the one who pushed her abductor out the window.

Some in the Macalister Clan glanced Chisholm's direction, but they seemed far more interested in what had become of their laird than in the three strangers riding into their village. Chisholm looked at each of the women desperate to find her, but Paisley was not among them. His next thought worried him more. Perhaps Macalister's men still held her captive or worse, Macalister sold her to someone else. His anxiety steadily increased as he dismounted and walked to the castle door.

Torn between their fear and their deep desire to know what would happen next, the brothers also dismounted, If all went well, they would have a glorious tale to tell -- seen firsthand -- if they lived through it, that is. Adair thought to draw his sword, but noticed no one was paying any particular attention to them and decided not to. Besides, his was not the best sword, what with it bent the way it was.

Chisholm banged on the door three times and even then no one in the courtyard paid any attention. Nor did anyone answer the door, so he walked into the growing crowd of followers near the crumpled body of their laird.

"Look at his face," a woman whispered. "Never have I seen a face so...befuddled."

"Poison," another mumbled.

"Nay," said a third. "His neck broke and that made his face sag."

Chisholm didn't care what killed him. Once more he looked around for Paisley and as he suspected, the MacDuff brothers were hanging back just watching. Then he looked up and spotted a woman standing in the window her laird had fallen out of. "Lass," he shouted, "What's become of Paisley MacGreagor?"

Rona quickly stepped back out of sight. She expected the MacGreagors to come for Paisley, but not so soon. If this one was Laird MacGreagor, he and his men might kill them all. Rona could think of no excuse not to answer and stuck her head back out the window. She looked, but the stranger seemed all alone and surely the MacGreagors would come with a mighty force of men. Perhaps they hid in the trees so she looked toward the forest, but saw nothing. Rona did however, spot the two MacDuff brothers whom she had seen before. "Gone," she finally answered.

Chisholm's heart sank. "Gone where?"

"She made off in the night."

Chisholm tried to see if there was honesty in the eyes of the woman, but she was too high up and he couldn't tell. "I will see for myself!"

"Come in then," Rona shouted. She turned, headed out of the room and down the stairs. Just as she arrived in the great hall, Macalister's second in command opened the door and let the three strangers in. "I will show you each room until you are satisfied the lass is not here."

Seated near the hearth, the old man said, "She run off in the night."

Chisholm walked to the old man and moved his hand up and down in front of his face. "You are blind?"

"Macalister blinded me and four others for looking at his wife's nakedness. I am blind, but I hear well enough and I could feel her in the room. The lass you seek went out the back door."

"Did Macalister's lads bring her here or did someone else?"

"You seem a might young to be her father," said Rona.

"I am not her father, I am Laird Graham. Her father is beside himself with worry and I must know, did Macalister marry her?"

"Nay, I killed him before..." She hadn't meant to say that. Alarmed, she glanced at each MacDuff brother and then stared into Chisholm's eyes.

"Pity, I hoped to kill him myself. If not you or me, her father would have."

Rona was terrified, but not at the mention of the MacGreagors. "Do you mean to tell the king?"

Chisholm remembered the brothers were right behind him listening to every word and knew as soon as they left, the gossip would begin and word would eventually reach the King of Scots ears. For a man to die at the hands of a woman in battle was one thing, but a woman who murdered a laird was something else again. "You might not have killed him. After all, he did take a bad fall out that window."

Rona was quick to follow his meaning. "That is true. I could not wake him is all and thought I might have given him bad wine for his evening meal."

"Bad wine?" Adair asked, moving up to stand beside Chisholm. "Is there such a thing as bad wine?"

Not to be out done by his brother, Ross moved up too. "I wish to know as well."

"Aye," Chisholm said, "If the grapes are yellow instead of green and the wine sits in the sun for a time, a lad can fall to his death on the spot."

"I knew that," said Ross.

This time it was Adair who shoved his brother, "You did not."

Suddenly the dog raced in the door and was about to wreck the place with his exuberance when Chisholm yelled, "Sit!"

The dog instantly obeyed and the brothers were astounded. They exchanged disbelieving glances and then Adair took a step closer to Chisholm and looked up. "Do we get the cows? We found her, this lass said we did."

"Aye, you will get the reward."

Adair shouted for joy, grabbed his brother's arm and pulled him back out the door. The dog paused just long enough to look at Chisholm, then at the brothers and back at Chisholm again, before he raced out the door and followed the brothers.

Chisholm could still hear their jubilation as they mounted their horses and rode out of the courtyard.

"Thank you," said Rona, "I feared you would have me executed."

"Where did Paisley go?"

"Behind the castle and then into the forest," the old man answered.

"Is she armed? Much can happen to a lass in the forest."

Rona quickly tried to comfort his worries. "I gave her my dagger but I did not trust any of the lads to take her, not that they would have, being so afraid of Macalister as they were.

"She is alone, then?"

"Aye," Rona said.

Chisholm was in a panic when he rushed out of the smelly castle and mounted his horse. He guided the stallion around the large structure, found the path Paisley had taken and rode into the forest. A few moments later, he halted. Paisley left in the night and the next night was approaching. Which way had she gone? The forest was vast and reached all the way to England in some areas. He decided to go as straight as possible and call her name often. Hopefully, she would recognize his voice, not be frightened and answer.

Much later, all he could report seeing was one hare, a red fox that spooked his horse and a golden eagle perched high in a tree. He neglected to ask if Paisley had food or water, and was tempted to go back. In the shadows of the tall trees, even he was having trouble knowing which direction he was going. The best thing to do, he decided, was to find a place to build a fire and hope Paisley would follow the smell of smoke -- if she could.

He left the castle in such a hurry he did not bother to ask if she was hurt. It would have been valuable information to have. The severity of the injury, if there was one, may well determine how far she could have walked. Then he remembered the old man tell of hearing her go, did not mention a limp and Chisholm began to breathe a little easier. Still, he had traveled on horseback much faster and farther than she could have on foot. She might not be injured, but she was definitely lost and alone.

The food he brought did not need cooking and it was a pity not to have something that would tempt a hungry Paisley to find him. Then again, he did have apples. Chisholm found a small clearing, dismounted and gathered enough wood to build a fire. He untied his sack, reached in, pulled out an apple and set it on a rock. Next, he found a stick, sharpened the end of it with his dagger and skewered the apple. He moved a rock near the small fire, looked around until he found another and put it on the other side. Then he balanced the stick between them and let the apple begin to slowly roast.

There was nothing to do but wait. Chisholm sat down, put his back against a tree and rested.

CHAPTER VII

In the Keith village, a converted barn complete with chickens and a hayloft served as the Keep. It was, after all, the largest building they had. The clan also had a high wooden fence made of tree limbs, tied together with leather strips, all the way around the small village. More tree limbs wedged against it both on the inside and out, kept it from falling and the two tall gates stood wide open.

A small scrap of hot cake was hardly enough to fill her empty stomach and Paisley hoped for a full meal. Although the clan seemed happy to see Blathan and his men, they did not seem friendly in her regard at all. No matter, she wouldn't be staying that long, but then she realized she wore Macalister colors and understood. The cottages were not adorned with flowers, tossed away food and horse droppings dotted the paths, and she took it to mean the people were not happy. Unhappy people would most likely mean she would be unhappy soon too.

When she mounted the horse behind Blathan she was glad to be off her feet, but after hours on a horse she was equally happy to be getting off. Once she had her balance, Blathan took hold of her arm and took her inside the Keep where Laird Keith waited. It took a moment for her eyes to adjust to the dimmer light, she could smell meat cooking and it increased her nagging hunger.

The table in the Keith great hall was nearly as wide as it was long and appeared to have at least one mended leg. The chairs were in no better repair and she wondered how they held the weight of the men. No wife or children were within, which Paisley thought odd, and at her feet a chicken pecked at bread crumbs on the floor. She was relieved when one of the men grabbed it and tossed the squawking bird out the door. Laird Keith, she noticed, was not a pleasant looking man and she hoped she would not be in his keeping for very long. He wore baggy long pants instead of a kilt, had two teeth missing and had not bothered to brush bread crumbs out of his blond beard.

At first when the men presented Laird Keith with the remarkable woman with glorious eyes, he thought of his own need of a wife. Yet when he walked to her and saw white hair at the top of her forehead, he yanked her scarf down and instantly flew into a rage.

Tired and hurting, Paisley jumped when he started to bellow unpleasant words in Gaelic, but that ended more quickly than she expected. Laird Keith abruptly lowered his voice and began to speak to Blathan in English. She pretended to concentrate on putting her scarf back over her hair, but she heard and understood every word.

"Take her back, Blathan!" Laird Keith insisted. "If she is discovered with us, we will all surely die. Have you not heard? She is MacGreagor's missing daughter, the one he offers a golden goblet for."

The color began to drain out of Blathan's face. "She said it was so, but I did not believe her. She wears a Macalister plaid."

"Good, then she will be found wearing it, only see she is not found alive."

Blathan was shocked. "What?"

"Do away with her!"

"Why?" Blathan glanced at Paisley, noticed her attention was focused on the chicken coming back in the door and turned back to face his laird.

Laird Keith put his hand on the back of his head as though it pained him. "I know MacGreagor and he will ride the whole of Scotland until he finds her. Once the deed is done, leave her where she will be found."

"But…"

"Dare you question me?"

Blathan lowered his eyes. "Nay."

His wife and children would have to wait, Blathan decided. He walked to her, took hold of Paisley's arm again and pulled her out the door. Then he let go and shouted for a fresh horse and supplies. As soon as they were brought to him, he mounted, allowed another man to lift her up behind him and turned to ride swiftly back through the open gates.

*

Where could she have gone, Chisholm wondered. The apple was starting to burn and still she had not come to him. He considered where she might go to look for water and wasn't certain even he would know how to find it without a horse. The foliage grew thickest near a water source, but in Scotland where it rained often, that bit of knowledge was of little value. He wondered if she knew how to drink the dew from the leaves of the trees, he wondered if she knew how to hunt, and most of all, he wondered if she might love him too.

She seemed to like him and he remembered how often he wanted to take her in his arms that night at the festival. She even watched him ride away and was still watching when he turned at the end of the glen and looked back. Would a woman who did not find him pleasing have done that?

When the stick holding the apple finally burned through and fell into the fire, he got up and kicked dirt until the flames went out. Perhaps when she found the forest so dense, she turned east or west. It would have been the prudent thing to do to find water, but which way did she go? If he chose incorrectly, he would widen the gap between them.

Chisholm sighed, bent down and picked a forest flower. One by one, he picked the five petals off; east, west, east, west…east. It was decided as well as anyone could decide, so he mounted his horse and headed east.

*

Not long after they left the land of the Keith, Blathan turned off the path and took Paisley into the forest. It would take more time to get to the place he had in mind, but at least there was less chance of anyone seeing them.

He was a conflicted man. Blathan had never killed a woman and certainly never one as beautiful as this. A pity it would be to do away with Paisley MacGreagor, a pity indeed. He thought about trading or even selling her, but then her body would not be found and Laird Keith would know.

More so on his mind was the question of where he could leave her so she was sure to be found. The forest would not do and out of the forest meant someone might see him do it. All men feared Justin

MacGreagor and he shuddered to think what would become of him if there was a witness.

He felt the woman slump against his back almost as soon as she wrapped her arms around him from behind and he felt sorry for her. An hour later he stopped and offered her a drink, which she thanked him for. She had not spoken much, but she looked very tired and that explained it. The sooner he put her out of her misery, the better. He put his flask away and urged the horse onward.

The forest again kept Paisley from knowing in which direction they traveled and with each passing moment, she felt she was coming closer and closer to her death. When she could bear it no longer she finally said, "Please do not kill me, I have harmed no one."

Blathan closed his eyes and bowed his head. She said it in English, must have heard every word and he could think of nothing to say. There would be no sneaking up on her to bash her over the head or slit her throat now. Instead, he may well be forced to look into her pleading eyes as he did it and the detestable thought made him wish he was in some far off land.

Paisley sat up a little straighter, shifted her weight and prayed she could talk him out of it. "I was lost, you found me and my father will be grateful."

"I must obey my laird."

"Must you? Have you never lied to him before?"

"He will know if you are found alive and he will kill me. What then will become of my wife and children?"

She sighed. "Then tell Laird Keith the truth. Tell him I will convince my father not to attack the Keiths and father will listen to me.

Besides, if you let me go, I shall probably die in the forest anyway…alone…lost and…"

"That will not do. Laird Keith is right; you must be left where someone will find you."

Paisley drew in a deep breath, "But if left alive, please say you will not leave me where Macalister can find me. It was he who had me taken and he who aimed to marry me against my will."

"Macalister is an evil man; I would rather kill you myself than leave you to his devices."

"I am truly grateful for that." Her scarf kept slipping back so she let go of her hold around his waist to retie it.

Abruptly, Blathan halted the horse and put a hand out to grab her in case she tried to slide down and run. He turned to look at her and once he realized what she was doing, he relaxed.

The woods were normally crawling with hunters, which meant someone was likely to see him kill her, and the color of her hair was certain to let men know who she was. "'Tis a curse," he muttered.

"What is?"

"Your hair."

"You cannot guess what a curse it is. Lads from all over Scotland have come to see me and I am often forced to hide." She finished tying her scarf, but did not wrap her arms around him again, not just yet. "You might tell Laird Keith I ran off and you could not find me."

He lowered his eyes and considered it. "'Tis a fine reward your father has offered to the lad who finds you. Has laird MacGreagor such a thing to give?"

She had never seen it, but Justin would not lie in such an

important case as this. "It is truly splendid."

"You have seen it?"

"Father does not display his wealth, even for his children to see, but I once saw it."

Blathan's eyes widened in wonder. "I would like to see it for myself."

"Take me home and I will see that the chalice is yours."

He turned a little more so he could see her better. "Aye, but then my laird would know I disobeyed, I could not go home and he would keep my wife and children from me.

"Oh, I see. He must be a very dreadful lad."

Blathan turned back around and lightly kicked the sides of his horse to make him move. "He cut my father down for no reason."

As soon as the horse began to walk again Paisley quickly put her arms back around Blathan and hung on. "And now he commands you to kill another lad's daughter. Do you know where my home is? I mean, which way it is?"

He raised his hand and pointed.

They were clearly not going toward her home and it was disappointing. Paying more attention now, she scanned the forest looking between the trees to see if anyone was watching. It occurred to her that if she let some of her hair show, it might just save her life. With one hand, she pulled the scarf to the front and made certain the back of her hair was uncovered.

Then she changed from English back to Gaelic in case someone could hear them. "Blathan, do you have a daughter?"

He was afraid she might mention that and closed his eyes. Having his daughter at a man's mercy bothered him greatly, yet he successfully pushed those thoughts away -- until now. "'Tis not the same."

"'Tis exactly the same," she argued. "You are to kill a lad's daughter. I was once little with loving arms I put around his strong neck when he lifted me. I do it still even now I am older. How he used to love swinging me around and how I loved it too. He often took all of us to play in a meadow. We are six brothers and sisters, you understand and..."

He let her keep talking, all the while growing closer and closer to the edge of the forest. When he could see the rolling hills through the trees, he halted his horse. "We will rest here."

Thrilled to be getting off the horse, Paisley made sure the scarf was covering the back of her hair, grabbed his arm and slid down. As soon as he dismounted, she asked him for a drink of water, took the flask he offered and tried to pull the plug out, but it was stuck. Using her most friendly smile, she said, "Can you not help me?"

He was a married man and he should not have found her so becoming, but even a married man has temptations. He took the flask, pulled out the plug, handed it back and stepped away. Killing her was going to be harder than he thought. When she returned his flask and asked, he watched her walk into the forest for her comfort.

Blathan kept thinking of his own daughter and soon realized he could not kill her. Instead, he would have to think of something to tell his laird later. He turned his back, folded his arms and hoped she would run off.

Escaping was Paisley's first thought and she kept walking further and further away. When she glanced back, the back of his head was still to her and she wondered if he meant for her to run. He had a horse, she did not and if he changed his mind and tried to find her, she could never outrun him. Her best hope was to hide in the bushes. She spotted thick undergrowth around a tree, eased behind it and crouched down to watch. At length, Blathan mounted his horse.

Paisley held her breath, but instead of coming for her, he headed back toward his village. For a very long time she waited, watched and listened, but Blathan did not come back.

She still had her dagger, but what she didn't have was food and water. She was free, alone and hungry, but at least now she knew which way to go. Paisley stood up, looked that direction and closed her eyes for a moment. If she tried to go straight, she would only get lost again. She remembered seeing flat lands through the trees and hoped by going back she could discern where she was.

Aware that Blathan could be hiding somewhere still determined to kill her, Paisley cautiously made her way back through the trees. She stopped to look between them often, listened for the sound of a horse coming her direction and when she had gone far enough, she could finally see the lush valleys and rolling hills of Scotland. While the quiet land was magnificent, what she wanted to see was a village full of people, who would not fear helping her.

Such was not to be, the land was completely void of life.

Still wary, she stepped out on the well-worn path that skirted the edge of the forest. There were no patches of tilled land and behind the rolling hills there were no mountains like the ones she had seen from Macalister's window. Two whole days had passed since she walked with Sawney in the MacGreagor glen.

Sawney…she was so consumed with her own problems, she had not worried about her brother or Rona all day, but then another thought occurred to her. Staying near the edge of the forest meant she could spot riders far away and if they were Macalisters she could always slip back in the trees and hide until they passed.

One thing though, which way was Macalister land? She slowly turned to look left, straight ahead, and then to her right. Surely a castle with four floors could be seen. Even so, the edge of the forest curved and she could not tell. She closed her eyes for a moment and tried to think. Had Blathan taken her east or west? Paisley was fairly certain she walked north when she entered the forest and east to find the Keith men. Yet Blathan did not take her back that direction, so he must have gone east or perhaps northeast to the Keith hold. But which way did he take her from there?

It was no use; she was too confused to figure it out. All she knew for certain was which way he pointed. She turned and started down the path she hoped would take her closer to home.

*

Justin and his thirty men arrived not more than two hours after Chisholm left. By then, Macalister's body was in a box with six men carrying him toward the graveyard.

From his position in the trees, Justin caught his breath. He looked at Shaw, who only shrugged and then at Ginnion.

"We do not know who is in the burial box," Ginnion tried, but he could tell Justin was not convinced.

"How many?" Justin asked, reluctantly turning his attention back to the village.

"Perhaps a hundred lads. 'Tis a very small clan. I count less than thirty cottages on this side of the castle," Shaw answered. "We cannot count the other side without showing ourselves."

"I see no stables and no piles of hay, Where are Macalister's horses?"

Shaw raised an eyebrow. "If we are very fortunate, there are no more cottages and the livestock grazes on the other side of the castle."

"Aye, if we are fortunate." Justin stared at the castle windows. "Were I to take a lass, I would keep her on the top floor with guards outside her door."

Ginnion nodded. "As would I. We could take all his people and demand a trade."

"Take them how?"

"Surround the village," Shaw answered. "If they try to fight, we will fight them, otherwise we will only keep them within."

"And if he hurts Paisley? A daft man does not take a lass and then easily give her back."

Ginnion, the commander of the warriors, thought hard about it and could not think of another way short of an all-out attack. An attack might also mean Paisley's death if they did not get inside the castle in time, and he doubted they could. He rubbed the side of his face and tried to think of another way.

"Perhaps we three have only come for a friendly visit," offered Justin. "Macalister does not know us and will perhaps not suspect."

Shaw shook his head, "He will know our colors and our size."

Justin puffed his cheeks. "What then?" Neither of his men

answered and he too was perplexed for a moment. "Macalister will expect us to attack, unless he is completely witless, but he will not expect us to show ourselves in his courtyard. Perhaps we should simply go in and ask him if he has her. Once we are inside, we can search. Tell the lads to go to the top floor first."

"Agreed," Shaw said. He spread the word, followed his laird out of the forest and down the path.

The Macalister clan was no different than the Kennedys and the Gunns. The sight of thirty-one heavily armed, very large men made them stop in their tracks afraid to move. There was one man, however, who instantly recognized the MacGreagor colors and slipped around the side of a cottage. He crouched down behind some bushes and hid.

Justin and his men ignored the people, rode into the courtyard and dismounted. Then Justin went to the door and gave it a mighty banging. When no one answered, he banged again. At last, the door opened, but the woman took one look at the size of the MacGreagors and tried to close it. Just in time, Shaw put a flat hand against the door and stopped the movement. As soon as he could feel no more resistance, he pushed the door wide open.

Rona quickly backed up. Her eyes were wide and her mouth had dropped open. She watched Justin's thirty men spread out to search the castle and her eyes widened even more when Justin walked toward her.

"Where is my daughter?"

"Gone," Rona managed to whisper.

"What?"

The giant's voice was as loud as his knock and she greatly feared him. She nervously cleared her throat and tried again. "Made off."

"When?"

"Last night," the old man shouted. He was getting a little tired of answering all the questions, especially those concerning Macalister's captive. For hours, every member of the clan wanted to know, came to ask and he was weary of the telling.

"Where is Macalister?"

The old man huffed, "Dead and soon buried, as he should be." He felt Rona walk up behind his chair and put her hands on his shoulders.

Justin took a forgotten breath. At least Paisley was not in the burial box. His men came to report from the kitchen, each shaking their heads and when the last of them came down the stairs without his daughter, he was convinced she wasn't there. "Where did she go?"

"Into the forest, would be my guess," the old man answered.

"Did she have water and food?"

"Nay," Rona admitted, "but I did give her my dagger."

"Why should I believe you?" Justin demanded.

A little more emboldened now, Rona put her hands on her hips. "Why would we chance lying to you? You would only come back and kill us all. Your daughter is no doubt half way home by now."

Justin was still not satisfied. "And the lad who took her from our glen? Where is he?"

For her brother's sake, Rona would lie. "I know not who took her. She was brought in while I was fetching food for the laird's dinner."

"If you have lied to me, I will surely be back."

There was nothing left to do but go into the forest and try to find her before she fell victim to another evil man, a wild boar, thirst or hunger. Justin turned and bolted back out the door. He was mounted and on his way up the village path by the time he shouted "Spread out." For the first of many times, he pursed his lips and sounded the whistle he knew Paisley would recognize.

*

Her decision to follow the edge of the forest was a good one for just when she needed water most, she found a shallow creek. She quickly knelt down, filled her hands with the cool, refreshing water and drank. Then she splashed her face and neck. It was time to rest but first, she stepped from rock to rock to get to the other side. The shade of the trees offered some measure of relief from the hot afternoon sun, but walking heightened her body heat and her exhaustion.

A large rock near the creek was the perfect place to sit and rest. Cautiously, she looked through the trees in every direction, decided she was safe and started to sit. Just then, something moved in the bushes and before she could draw her dagger, the biggest dog she had ever seen raced forward, jumped into her lap and knocked her backwards into the creek.

Paisley began to laugh. Not a second later, the rambunctious dog was on top of her trying his best to lick her face. "At last, a friend!" Distracted finally by something he spotted in the water, the dog started off down the stream into the open meadow.

She didn't mind getting wet, in fact, it felt good and it was the closest thing to a bath she was probably going to get for a while. She sat up, languished in the feel of the water washing over her lap, washed her face and arms, and took another look at the scratches on her legs. Then she got up and waded out of the water.

The dog was back but this time she was prepared and said, "Sit," and when the dog lay down and rolled over on his back instead, she giggled. There was no resisting him, so she leaned down and rubbed his belly. Instantly, his hind leg began to jerk his delight. As soon as she stopped, the dog was up and running again, only this time into the forest.

Seeing him disappear depressed her a little. "Dog, come back dog!" She waited but he did not come back. Paisley was alone again and it upset her. Once more she stepped out onto the path and looked around. Ginnion taught her to follow the creek to find people, but that meant walking in the meadow where Macalister could see her. Soon she would lose the better daylight, so instead of resting, she decided she best keep going. There had to be people somewhere.

CHAPTER VIII

The evening meal in the MacGreagor great hall was a somber affair. Another night was upon them with no word of Paisley or Justin and the men.

The guards and hunters came as soon as they returned home to report to Carley's husband, Moan, but they had very little to say. The hunters often met hunters or warriors from other clans on the paths and there was nearly always some rumor to report. Save for the MacGreagors telling of Paisley's abduction and the reward, the clans seemed to have no other news.

MacGreagor warriors found no trace of her in the woods after yet another search and felt they had combed every inch. Their captive was still not talking, nor was he being given food or water just as their laird commanded. The stable near the Keep, housed only the mounts belonging to Justin's top men and was now void of horses. All the grain and possible food sources had been removed as had any wooden buckets with even a single drop of water. Still, the man refused to utter a word.

The long table in the Keep seemed empty with most all the men in the family gone. Justin's sons, his sisters and enough children to fill any normal sized room ate their meal quietly. Blanka tried twice to start a happy conversation but her attempts fell flat.

The air was still too warm, everyone was exhausted and when

Blanka walked outside, she was not surprised to find Thomas waiting for her. She went to him, leaned against the short stonewall he sat on and let the cool evening breeze blow against her face. Even Thomas did not seem to want to talk and she did not mind. Just being with him felt normal and comforting.

Half the usual number of guards stood in the glen and watched the trees, but most of the women and children had gone home and there were few to worry over. Blanka could feel Thomas look at her occasionally as though he wanted to say something, but he did not speak. Still, when she looked at him, he turned her way, gently moved a lock of loose hair away from her face and when she smiled, so did he.

*

Chisholm was becoming more worried by the moment. He called her name often, wove his horse around bushes and ferns and kept searching. The forest was growing dark again and he greatly feared for her. If she managed to survive one night, could she do it again? Several times he halted his horse just to listen or reconsider his choice of directions, but he heard nothing unusual and could not think of a better direction.

He missed her, he even loved her, he was determined to find her and he would keep looking if it took him an eternity.

*

Justin was just as frustrated. His men fanned out as soon as they entered the forest with Ginnion on one end of the fan and Shaw on the other. They had become a moving semicircle, looking around every tree and behind every bush trying to find her. Yet the whistle he longed to hear in return did not come and soon they would need to stop and rest the horses before they killed them.

To Justin, Paisley was still that little girl who loved to hug his neck or curl up in his lap when she was tired. It was something he allowed all his children to do, even in the great hall when he was busy. It wasn't much, but the demands of the clan offered too little time to let his children feel his love otherwise. Now the most loving child of all was lost somewhere in a forest and he could not find her. His rage had turned to fear for her and after hours of looking, his heart began to hurt.

*

Suddenly, Chisholm saw movement in the bushes up ahead. He swung down off his horse, drew his weapon, prepared himself to fight and waited. He didn't have to wait long; Mutton stuck his head out from behind the bush. Only this time, he did not try to jump up on Chisholm or give his normal overwhelming greeting. Instead, the dog stopped, looked at him and barked.

"What?" Chisholm asked.

The dog swiftly turned around and started off, but then he stopped again and when Chisholm was not following, he went back. Again he barked, and when that didn't work, he showed his teeth and growled.

"What is the matter with you?" He watched the dog turn his head to one side. "Are the brothers hurt?" He didn't want to give up the search for Paisley, but the dog obviously wanted him to follow. Perhaps this would not take too long and then he could set out again. He put his weapon away and got back on his horse.

*

Paisley couldn't remember a time when she needed food and sleep more. She realized she had not rested for very long beside the creek and each step was beginning to feel like there were weights on her feet. Still there was no sign of human existence anywhere, not a cow, a horse or even a lost sheep.

"Macalister probably scared even the animals away." She did not realize she was talking to herself and did not care.

The setting of the sun would soon surround her with the dimmer light and she regretted it. The heat of the day dried her clothing, which she also regretted since they were cooler wet, but the one thing that annoyed her most was the scarf on her head. It kept trying to slide back and at last, she stopped, untied it, pulled it off and released her long hair. Then she looked for a way to carry it so her hands would still be free. She thought to tie it around her waist, but that would make drawing her dagger quickly less possible. She could tie it around her neck, she decided. She wrapped it around, pulled her hair out and was starting to tie it in front when she looked up.

Just beyond the trees sat a man on a horse with a dog sitting quietly beside him. She had not heard a thing, gasped and was about to turn and run when she saw his necklace. Slowly, she raised her gaze, looked at his face, covered her mouth and started to cry.

Chisholm walked his horse up beside her, bent down, waited for her to wrap her arms around his neck and then lifted her into his lap. She didn't quickly let go and he didn't want her to. When she did, she wrapped her arms around his torso, laid her head against his chest and began to sob. Never in his life had he felt anything as magnificent as having the woman he loved safe in his arms. For a long time he just held her tight and stroked the back of her hair.

"Macalister is dead," he whispered.

It was all she could do to nod.

He let her cry a little while longer and then decided her tears might never stop if he did not distract her. "I am so happy to see you, are you hurt?"

She pulled away just enough to lift her head and point at the bruise under her chin, and then she went back into the comfort of his arms.

"Did someone do this?" Her nod made him furious, but he set that aside for later. "You are safe now."

"I was so very frightened," she managed to whisper.

"I know, but you need not be frightened any longer."

At length, she took a deep breath and tried to stop crying. When he handed her his cloth, she let go, sat up straight and wiped the tears away. "I need a bath."

It made him smile, but letting her bathe was the last thing on his mind. "Are you hungry?"

She quickly nodded. "It has been a long time since my last meal."

"I brought cheese, bread and apples. Which would you like first?"

"All of them."

Chisholm chuckled. "All I have is yours."

"Wait, 'tis hard to chew. Can you cut small pieces?"

"I can and I will let you down if you promise not to try to run off."

She wiped the last of her tears away and rolled her eyes. "I wish to never be alone in the forest again." She took hold of his arm and slid down off the horse. An instant later, the dog was about to pounce again, but Chisholm dismounted just in time to stop him.

"This is, Mutton," he said, beginning to untie the strings of his food sack.

She was incredulous. "You named your dog, Mutton?"

"Not I, 'tis the MacDuff brothers who named him."

Paisley grinned, "That, I can believe. Mutton knocked me into the creek earlier."

"You know the MacDuff brothers, Adair and Ross?"

"They are constantly watching us from the trees in the glen, but they are harmless and we pay them no mind."

"Mutton helped me find you."

She reached down with both hands and started rubbing the dog behind his ears, "Then he is the best dog in all the world and I shall remember to thank the MacDuff brothers when I am home."

"Sit down, Paisley, you are tired."

"I confess I am. She looked around for a place to sit, found a tree stump and gladly took the weight off her feet.

Chisholm reached into his sack, pulled out the cheese, folded the cloth back and pulled his dagger. He cut a thin slice and handed it to her. "Who hit you?"

"I do not know his name." Eagerly, she broke off a small bite, put it in her mouth and savored the taste as it melted and softened."

Sitting quietly as he was told, the dog ignored the horse as it wandered into the meadow to graze, looked at her and then at Chisholm. Again he looked at Paisley, but neither seemed interested in tossing a morsel his way.

"I would like a word with the lad who took you," said Chisholm.

"My father will kill him."

"Not if I kill him first."

Paisley stopped eating and looked up at him. "I wish to go home; can you not put off the killing until later?" Then she suddenly remembered, "Sawney?"

"He is fine. A small cut on his neck, but it will heal."

She drew in a deep breath and truly relaxed for the first time in two days. "Who killed Macalister?"

"A lass said she did. I believe she is the one who helped you escape."

"Rona is alive then. Macalister threatened to kill her if I did not obey."

Realizing he was not going to get fed, the dog finally raced off to find his own meal.

"Just as I arrived, Macalister came flying out a window." He watched Paisley's eyes light up and continued. "A lass in the crowd said he had the look of someone poisoned."

"Poison, how clever of Rona." She took the next slice of cheese he handed her and began to break it into small bites as well. Then she watched him put the cheese away, produce a loaf of bread and break off part.

"Paisley, was there nothing odd about the lad who took you? A scar perhaps or…"

She quickly swallowed. "There were two of them."

"Aye, Sawney overtook one, but the lad would not tell us who the other one was. He only said he was forced to do it or his family would die."

"'Tis likely true."

Chisholm thought about that. "Perhaps I might take a lass if my laird demanded it and threatened to hurt my family."

"So would I. I am not *that* injured and Macalister said the lad only hit me to keep me from screaming."

Chisholm didn't think Justin would accept that excuse, but decided to change the subject. "Macalister's clan seemed pleased their laird was dead."

Paisley put a small chunk of bread in her mouth and savored the taste a moment before she swallowed. "The wife he killed was Rona's sister." Embarrassed suddenly, she timidly continued, "Perhaps someday I shall tell you what she did to deserve his ire."

"You cannot tell me now?" Chisholm already knew why the old man was blinded and guessed it was the same reason Macalister killed his wife, but he enjoyed Paisley's blush.

"'Tis shameful."

"Would you tell a husband?"

She thought his question leading, looked down and broke off another bite of bread. "There are many husbands in our clan and I cannot think of a one I would tell."

Chisholm should have, but did not expect her to avoid the subject so expertly. She left him with no response, so he let her eat in silence for a while. "When you have eaten, would you like to stay the night or shall we keep going?"

"My father must be beside himself with worry. For his sake we should keep going."

"Done then. Are you full or will you want an apple?"

"I fear an apple too painful to chew. Perhaps later."

He walked to her, knelt down, examined her bruise more closely and stood back up. "Tell me true, have you any other injuries?"

He looked worried, so she tried to comfort him. "My feet hurt from walking, my legs have suffered thorns from the bushes and a rock or two in the creek might have bruised my back, but I will mend. What I want most is a bath." She ate the last crumb of bread and brushed her hands. "How far from home are we?"

"Perhaps half a day, but we can travel long. First, we must rest this tired old horse a while." He cut another slice of cheese and when she only took half, he put the other half in his own mouth. He had not thought of eating for quite some time, he realized. Paisley looked awful and he was torn between letting her rest and getting her home faster. It was improper for a man and woman to stay the night alone together, but he doubted Justin would kill him for it.

Chisholm ate his fill and put the food away. Then he crossed his feet at the ankles and sat down on the ground in front of her. "Are your teeth broken?"

She quickly ran her tongue over her top and bottom teeth. "I do not think so."

"Do you want to tell me what happened?" She shook her head and he wondered if it was because of something too awful to tell, or if talking hurt her too much. "Perhaps you should lie down and rest for a time."

"If you do not let me fall, I can rest on the horse."

Chisholm smiled, "I will not let you fall." She was determined to go home and he could not blame her for that.

*

In the distance, Justin heard the whistle that told the men to stop and rest. He would have preferred to keep going, suspected it was Shaw who began the whistle and had to admit it was probably time. He noticed the two men nearest him come to give their laird protection and got down off his horse. It was good to walk, the horses had ample foliage to feed on and the forest was getting dark. One of the men handed him an apple and Justin absentmindedly bit into it. Resting the horses for an hour or so meant another hour Paisley was lost and perhaps hurt.

One of the men with him whistled, his whistles were returned and soon two more men came, followed by two more until Justin found himself surrounded by all his men. Each was just as tired and worried as he was. He waited until they settled down and ate something before he said, "I will hear your suggestions now."

Shaw puffed his cheeks. "I can think of nothing."

"Nor I," agreed Ginnion and noticed several others nod.

Finally, Andrew spoke up. "I watched Paisley grow up and she is far more clever than you think. I once saw her outwit three older laddies and..."

"Andrew," said Justin, "what are you trying to say?"

"Just that I do not think she would stay in the forest for a second night."

Justin looked down and began to thoughtfully rub his forehead again. "Where would she go?"

"She would know she was lost and perhaps go back." Ginnion said.

"And let Macalister capture her again? I hardly think that likely," argued Justin.

Shaw stretched his body one way and then the other to loosen his tired muscles. "Unless she knew Macalister was dead."

Ginnion's eyes brightened, "She knows how to kill a man, perhaps Macalister captured a lass he did not have the wits to fear."

"I would fear any MacGreagor lass. She can look into your eyes, smile her sweetest smile and stab your heart before you see her hand move," said Andrew. Some of the men snickered and he decided he had said enough.

Justin considered it. "Paisley killed Macalister, the lass helped her flee and she went into the forest for her safety. Then what would she do?"

"She would stay the night, satisfy herself no one was chasing her and then go back."

"To the castle?"

"Nay, to the path along the edge of the forest."

"The one we took to get to the castle? We did not see her there."

"Well," Shaw started, "Perhaps she did not know which way to go?"

"Or perhaps she did not go back to the path at all."

"Or someone else took…" Ginnion glanced at Justin's alarm and decided not to finish that sentence.

"We have no choice then. Ten will keep searching the forest, ten will take the path toward home and ten will go the other way. If she can, she will hear our whistles and answer."

"Which way will you go?"

Justin finally sat down on a fallen log and put his face in his hands. "I am too tired to decide."

"Then we will sleep and decide in the morning. We cannot find her in the dark anyway."

At last Justin nodded and the men set their horses free, began to spread their plaids and bed down. "The lads on guard will whistle still?"

Every one of his men said, "Aye."

The whistles were both a comfort and a bother. Each time they sounded, Justin stayed awake to see if she would answer. When she didn't he again felt old and useless before he drifted back to sleep.

*

Chisholm was tired too. He could not remember the last truly good night's sleep he'd had and the woman in his arms with her back to him was heavy against his chest. He kept his horse on the path, tried to watch for strangers or wild animals and kept going. Then he began to worry something more than just exhaustion was wrong with her. It was too much. Just as he was about to stop, she stirred and sat up.

"Are you hurting?"

She nodded, so he halted his horse and swung down. Then he put his hands on her waist, waited for her to put hers on his shoulders and lifted her down. He heard her slightly moan, held on until she got her balance and then held on a little longer. "Are you crying?"

"Nay, it is just that I hurt everywhere."

He let go finally, and started to untie his flask, "Fortunately, you have not yet drunk all the wine."

Just then, they heard someone whistle. Paisley excitedly looked up at him. "MacGreagors, they have found us. Whistle back."

He did as she said.

*

Shaw had not let his horse wander away, had not slept a wink and when he heard the faint whistle in the distance, he was up like a bolt of lightning. He untied his horse and mounted before the others even had a chance to sit up. "Paisley," he yelled as he urged his horse through the forest. Behind him, he heard Justin call for his horse.

*

Chisholm waited and when he heard the whistle again he looked down to see Paisley's relieved smile. He returned the whistle, realized it might be his last chance to hold her, and when she put her hand on his arm, he could not resist. He cupped one hand around the back of her head, wrapped the other around her waist and pulled her to him. She did not resist and put her arms around him as well when he laid his head against the top of hers. Nevertheless, the last thing he needed was for a MacGreagor to find him holding her. Reluctantly, he moved back.

She regretted letting go too, but she understood and took two steps away from him as well. A third whistle sounded only this time closer and her excitement steadily grew. After another two whistle exchanges, Shaw swung down off his horse, swooped Paisley off the ground and began kissing her neck until she giggled. Then he noticed her bruise and his smile turned to horror. "I have hurt you."

She hugged his neck, "Your kisses can never hurt me. Is Father with you?"

"Aye and I best let him know where you are or he will have my head." He gently hugged her one more time and set her down. Then he let out a low, long whistle and listened to it being repeated several times in the forest. The whistle meant the danger was over and he knew Justin would be greatly relieved.

"How many has he brought?" Paisley asked.

"Thirty, but only because Ginnion talked your father out of bringing them all." Shaw playfully slapped Chisholm on the back, "Fancy finding you here." He started another round of whistles so the others could find them, sat down near a tree and began to untie the leather straps that laced from his shoe to his knee. Then he dumped two pebbles out of his shoe and put it back on. "Macalister is dead."

"So I heard," she answered. "Uncle, I need a bath."

"Can it wait until you get home or shall we find a loch to toss you in?"

"Uncle, look out!"

It was too late. Happy to greet yet another unsuspecting person, Mutton dashed out of the bushes and flew into Shaw's lap. Shaw threw out both his arms and caught himself just in time to keep from falling over, and then he glared at the dog. Mutton was not deterred in the least and tried to lick Shaw's face, so Shaw pushed him away and glared at his giggling niece instead.

Finally, Chisholm took pity and made the dog sit. Mutton didn't sit long before he sped off into the dimly lit meadow.

Shaw laced up his shoes and glanced up. Behind Paisley, Justin sat on his horse and looked as though he could not move. It was not until she turned around that Justin lifted his leg over, got down and opened his arms to her.

She gladly went into them and held him as tight as she still had the strength to. Again she was crying and it frustrated her, "I feared never seeing you again."

"I feared the same." He kissed the top of her head, held her back so he could look at her face and was about to lift her chin.

Just in time, Chisholm grabbed Justin's hand. "She is hurt."

Justin wrinkled his brow. He turned his head to the side, looked under her chin and winced. "I will kill the lad who did this."

"Aye, but later, father. I want to go home and the sooner the better."

"Aye, we must go home very soon," said Ginnion, quietly riding up behind Justin. "Your father has a bride waiting."

Paisley was astounded and Justin rolled his eyes. "I will explain it later." He had forgotten all about Blanka and just about everything else. "Have you eaten, have you other injuries, are…"

She put her hand on his arm to calm him. "Laird Graham fed me, but if you have wine I could use a little more for my pain. I did not prefer Macalister's wine, it was bitter."

Justin quickly untied his flask and helped her drink while the rest of his thirty men arrived, each with a smile on his face. Before he had a chance to tie his flask back on, she leaned forward and slumped against him. He wrapped an arm around her to hold her up, handed the flask to Ginnion, put his other arm under her legs and picked her up. Then he looked at Chisholm. "Has she other complaints?"

"She said her feet hurt, the dog knocked her in the creek and her legs were cut from walking through the bushes, but that is all."

Shaw quickly spread a plaid on the ground so Justin could lay her down, then he said, "Look away, lads." Worried, they did as they were told, but none were more worried than Chisholm.

While Shaw and Ginnion got a good look at her arms, Justin examined each leg. One scratch was deeper than the others, but it was not red and hot. He looked for bites too, and then he took off her shoes. The bottoms of her feet were red and swollen, but she did not have any cuts. Next, he sat her up and held her while Shaw pulled the shirt out of her belt and looked at her back.

"She has two large bruises, but the skin is not broken."

Shaw was about to tuck her shirt back under her belt when she moaned, so he moved away so Justin could lay her back down. "She is tired, Justin."

"Aye, we are all tired. We will let her sleep and take her home in the morning."

Shaw raised an eyebrow. "She asked for a bath. Three days without a bath and she will never forgive us." He took the plaid Essen handed him, made sure she was covered and told the men they could look.

"If a bath is her biggest complaint, I am well pleased," said Justin. Then he looked at Ginnion. "We will stay the night. Let the horses rest and then send two men home to tell them she is found. We will take the path that leads to the river. Lads are to bring her sister with clean clothes and soap to meet us there. Then she can bathe in the river and change into MacGreagor colors before she is seen."

*

Paisley was sound asleep and did not wake when she was moved out of the trees into the meadow where the men could guard her better.

The MacGreagor horses wandered off to graze, the men built a fire and then sat or stood in a circle around her, all but the two who hurried off to notify the clan. Justin sat near her head to comfort her if she woke and Chisholm took up a sitting position near her feet while Shaw, Ginnion and Essen, her uncles, rested nearby.

Justin hoped she would wake at the smell of food cooking and glanced at her often, but even that did not disturb her. There was nothing left to do but talk and it was to Chisholm he wanted to talk most. "How did you find her?"

Chisholm told of the brothers and watching Macalister's body fly out the window. He described his search, the dog's help and then added, "She cried when I found her."

"Aye, her eyes are still red from crying. You are a good lad, Graham. Have you your heart set on my daughter?"

Chisholm was surprised by Justin's directness. "Once I suspected the brothers knew where she was, I left with all haste and neglected even to bring my guard."

Justin smiled. "Does she prefer you?"

"Not yet, but I am hopeful."

"Sawney will know, we shall ask him when we get home."

"I must return to my home first...if I still have a home. I have neglected everything to find her and do not recall even leaving anyone in command. They must think me daft by now."

"Love makes a lad daft; at least that is what they say about me."

Chisholm grinned. "I would have liked seeing that."

"It was not a pleasant sight, I assure you." Each man was lost in his own thoughts for a moment and when Paisley began to stir, they both paid attention to her. She moaned, changed positions a little and closed her eyes again.

Justin waited a while longer before he broke the silence. "How did she get here? She was lost, but I cannot understand it. She left Macalister's castle and entered the forest going north, which was the right direction to get home. So how has she come to be east instead?"

Chisholm thought about that for a moment. "She was going back toward the castle when I found her. Perhaps she walked in circles."

"You must be right."

Paisley did not go back to sleep as they thought and although her father was clearly puzzled, she was determined not to betray Blathan. It would be hard enough for him when Laird Keith learned she was alive. On the other hand, he let her escape and if she could protect him somehow, she surely should. But how? If her father knew Laird Keith wanted her dead, he would be enraged and might even attack their village. If that happened, Blathan would surely be killed. No, it was best not to mention it.

"You will wake the dead with all your talking," she finally complained.

Justin smiled and reached out to touch her shoulder. "Forgive us. Are you hurting, do you want more wine?"

She thought that a fine idea and when she struggled to sit up, she took hold of the hand Chisholm offered her. "Thank you." She tried to smile, but her jaw hurt even more than the day before, she let go of his hand and cupped it under her chin. "I hurt everywhere."

"I know, but more sleep will make it better." Justin unplugged the stopper of the wine flask Ginnion handed him and helped her drink until she pushed it away with her hand.

A tear rolled down her cheek. "I could not find water and when I did finally, I remembered Ginnion said to follow it downhill, but when I got to the edge of the forest, there were no people."

"I am so sorry," Justin said. "Can you sleep now?"

She nodded and lay back down. Hopefully, Justin would be satisfied with her explanation and the Keith village would be safe. On the other hand, Blathan might not be, but she was too tired to worry about that just now.

Justin pulled her cover up and tucked it around her. It was time they all slept and being as quiet as they could, Justin spread his plaid out on one side of her while Chisholm put his on the other side.

As soon as he got settled, Paisley turned her head toward Chisholm. "What have you done with my favorite dog?"

Chisholm smiled and turned on his side to face her. "I believe he licked the face of every lad here and then ran off."

She giggled, closed her eyes and went back to sleep.

Even with her swollen jaw, she was still the most beautiful woman he had ever seen and he was determined to make her his wife. Time, he reminded himself, she needs time to heal. Exhausted himself, it wasn't long before he too was sound asleep.

CHAPTER IX

"She is found!" came the shouts of the men who rode swiftly into the MacGreagor glen the next morning. Soon everyone was rejoicing and could not wait to question the men -- Is she hurt, was there a war and when will they arrive?

The entire clan was delighted to hear their men, their laird and his daughter would soon be arriving -- all but Blanka and Thomas. In the courtyard with the gathering crowd, Thomas folded his arms and just watched. Blanka found an empty place next to him, folded her arms and watched Thomas more often than the happy crowd.

There had to be a way out of her mess and perhaps there was, if Thomas felt the same as she. Only he said nothing, did not leave his hand in hers longer than was necessary and she could not be sure. Yet, she felt his warmth when they were together instead of the cold reserve of her father's guards, and hoped she did not mistake his meaning. Then again, all the MacGreagor men seemed uncommonly friendly and helpful. Perhaps she felt his warmth because she so desperately wanted to. It was all very confusing. Now, Justin was coming home and perhaps he would want to walk with her instead, in the tradition of courtships. "Will you walk with me?" she asked him finally.

The cool morning air felt wonderful after yet another hot night and Thomas was happy she asked. She chose to walk the path beside the river this time and although she might have been in a little more danger than in the glen, he did not object. They walked in silence only because he could think of nothing to say.

"You are very quiet this day. Is something amiss?" she asked.

He liked the sound of the rushing water, the smell of the air away from the smoke of the hearths and most of all, he liked being with her. It was an honor to protect her but dangerous to fall in love with a woman who might well be his laird's next wife. "Nothing is amiss. I enjoy quiet occasionally and once Paisley is recovered, we'll not likely be able to hear ourselves think."

Blanka smiled. "I look forward to that." She bent down and when she did, she reached for his hand to keep from falling. Then she picked up a small blue rock and examined it. As though she had not noticed the feel of her hand in his, she let go and went to the edge of the river. Kneeling down, she washed the rock in the edge of the water and once more took his hand when he offered it to help her stand up.

Thomas was not pleased. The last thing he needed was for her to touch him and the temptation to take her in his arms was becoming a plague on his mind. But what could he do? It was normal and natural to give his hand to her whenever she needed it. Save for meals, he had been with her constantly, walking, sitting on the logs near the graveyard under the shade of the trees, or watching the children play in the courtyard where the two of them could sit on the short wall together. He liked her smile, loved her laughter and even appreciated the way she liked to tease him. It was almost as if she fancied him as well.

"What do you do, I mean when you are not with me."

"I am a hunter."

"A hunter? Then you know these woods very well. Justin's sister said there is a waterfall not far away. Is it so?"

"Aye, but it is not safe there, at least not just now."

She flashed her smile at him. "But when it is safe, will you take me."

He truly wanted to and would if given the chance, but he had to wait until Justin came home and who knew what that might mean? "If it is permitted," he managed to mutter.

"Permitted by your laird?"

"Aye."

She sighed and kept strolling down the path. "I am torn."

"How so?"

"I want very much for your Paisley to be safe, but I do not look forward to your laird's return."

"Will your father force you to marry him?"

Blanka looked away for a moment. "He will try, but as I said, I will not welcome it. A life with that sort of husband is much more demanding than most. 'Tis hard enough being the daughter of a laird. Did your parents take you to run and play in a meadow, perhaps with a noon meal and plenty to drink?"

"Aye, they took us often."

"I have never been."

He stopped and looked at her to see if she was teasing him. "Never?"

"Not even once. Father always had much to do. How I longed to put out my arms and spin around and around in the pleasant meadows where wildflowers grow. I dreamed of seeing rabbits hop, or a deer with her fawn, or even a red fox. I have seen none of those, save after they are dead, and even if Father had taken us, we would have been surrounded by lads to protect us."

Thomas was reminded of his duties, glanced around to make certain they were safe before he said, "Have you never seen a waterfall?"

"Once, but it was on our way here and father would not let us linger. We filled our flasks and moved on. There is no arguing with my father."

"Aye, but a laird must be stern to keep his clan under his command."

"Not *that* stern. Even if it is necessary, I do not wish it on my children. I want them to run and play, do their mischief and then watch them sleep peacefully at night. My mother is required to be with Father the whole evening through and she often complains of missing our youth."

"You would prefer a candle maker, a tanner or even a hunter?" Thomas asked.

"I care not what he does as long as he loves me."

"Yet you are kind and you do not withhold your smiles. You will make a good mistress."

"Perhaps, but her smile fades when a lass is miserable. At least my mother's has. I could never be happy with a lad who is forced to consider me, by a father who believes he does the right thing. My father is wrong and I care not to pay the price for his error."

"But will you be able to talk your father out of it?"

"He will not listen to me, he never has before. I am condemned unless your laird does not prefer me." She started them walking again. "Perhaps I might grow a longer nose or put some sort of unsightly mole on the end of it. There is always…"

She was making him laugh on the outside, but inside he was miserable. There had to be a way to claim her and just now he decided he would, even if he had to face an upset Justin to do it.

*

Still in the meadow surrounded by men, Paisley abruptly sat up and loudly said, "I do not want to die."

She frightened the men, who quickly looked around to see what the danger was, but there were no intruders or wild animals.

Justin quickly took her in his arms. "You are safe, Paisley. 'Tis only a bad dream."

Her heart was pounding and she struggled to calm her labored breathing. In her dream, Blathan had Macalister's eyes, was holding a blade to her neck and starting to cut. At length, she closed her eyes and relaxed against her father. "I am sorry, Father, I did not mean to wake you."

"Perhaps more wine will help you go back to sleep."

"I thirst, but for water," she whispered. "I fear I will never get enough water."

Justin looked around and accepted the flask of water a wide-awake Chisholm handed him.

As soon as she finished drinking, she relaxed against her father again. "Is Sawney truly well?"

"Truly, he was very brave, for a laddie his age. Do you wish to tell me about your dream?" She shook her head, so he tried again. "You liked telling me well enough when you were a wee babe."

Again she shook her head. "I only want to bathe and sleep in my own bed. Can we not get an early start?"

Justin smiled. It was not that early. "It appears everyone is awake." He looked at his men and when several nodded, he kissed her forehead. "Will the ride hurt you?"

"Not if she rides with you," Shaw put in, beginning to fold his plaid. "You are getting old and your chest is softer."

Justin glared at Shaw, but the men laughed and even Paisley managed to giggle.

*

Thomas and Blanka were back in time to watch two MacGreagor warriors and Leslie ride out to meet Paisley at the river. Neither of them had a solution to the problem and neither managed to tell the other how they felt, but it was there; the feeling of closeness and belonging, and both of them knew it.

*

Paisley was disturbed. The ride seated in front of Justin on the jostling horse with one leg on each side was uncomfortable at best, especially after so many hours on Blathan's horse. Normally, she would have loved seeing the forest on both sides of the path, watching the birds in the air and smelling the pine trees. She would also have been proud to be with so many hearty MacGreagor warriors, but what to do, to help Blathan plagued her mind.

Twice, she looked back to make sure Chisholm was still with them and when they finally reached the path that would take him home, she made Justin stop. She got off the horse and as she walked back through the line of men, she saw him dismount as well.

Without thinking, she started to touch him and then dropped her hand. "Thank you, I shall never forget." Realizing everyone was watching her, she lowered her eyes. "Will you come again? I was not there to greet you the last time."

"I will be honored." He wanted to show her how much, but he slightly bowed instead and got back on his horse. He turned his steed around to get one more look at her before he hurried up the path toward his home. He would return soon, furthermore, he was encouraged enough to believe she loved him too.

*

The MacGreagors finished riding through the narrow valley between two hills and were about to go around the last curve in the path before reaching the river when Paisley suddenly said, "Father, please stop."

He immediately halted the men and his horse. "Are you hurting?"

"Aye," she answered, "but I need my comfort more."

"Spread out," Justin shouted. He found a place out of sight in the woods where he thought she would be safe and then left her alone.

"Blathan," she whispered. "What about Blathan?" The thought of him dying at the hands of Laird Keith, because he let her live, upset her even more than it had in the night, and she had thought of little else. Soon the clan would see her alive, gossip would quickly spread, if it hadn't already, and how long could it be before Laird Keith guessed his order had been disobeyed? At length, she walked back to her father.

She drank from the flask he offered her, carefully wiped the spillage off her painful chin and looked up at him. "Promise you will not attack."

Justin was taken aback. "Macalister is dead, I have no cause to attack save for the lad who took you."

She hesitated, but it had to be said, "There was another. Promise you will let him live."

"Who?"

By then, all her uncles were within hearing. "Father, please promise me first. There was one who helped me and I do not wish him to die."

Justin feared what he was about to hear and was reluctant to agree, but he nodded.

It was the first time she noticed her scarf was gone, but she dismissed that worry. "In the forest I happened upon a few Keith warriors. They thought Macalister sent me to spy on them and even though I told them who I was, and that I was lost, they did not believe me. They took me to their village to see what their laird said to do with me. Blathan is the name of the lad who saved me"

"They took you east," said Justin.

"Aye." She stopped and took a couple of steps away from her father to collect her thoughts. "I wore my scarf and when Laird Keith took it off and discovered the color of my hair, he was enraged. He shouted at Blathan in English, which he supposed I did not understand." Again she stopped and took another two steps away. Justin liked to pace when he was upset and everyone knew not to get in his way.

"Go on, why was Keith enraged?"

"He said you would think he took me and attack his village. So he…"

"He what, Paisley?"

She lightly bit her lip and hesitated, but it had to be said. "He told Blathan to kill me and leave my body where it would be discovered." She could see the rage building in her father's eyes and quickly went on. "But Father, Blathan disobeyed. He even turned his back so I could run off. If you attack the Keith village, you might kill him by mistake - - if his laird has not already killed him. He disobeyed a command and as soon as Laird Keith hears I am alive…" She let her words fall away and watched to see what her father would do.

Justin looked at Shaw and then calmed himself for her sake. "Why did Keith want your body found?"

"So you would stop looking and never suspect him."

Shaw rolled his eyes. "As if no one would ever tell of a strange lass brought to him and then taken away."

That was something Paisley had not considered. "Wearing a green scarf and Macalister colors," she added. Then she looked at her father again. "You would have heard anyway, so he ordered my death for nothing."

"Aye, he is a foolish lad," said Justin. "What would you have me do to help this Blathan?"

"I do not know, what can be done? Surely he is in danger and he has a wife and children."

Justin went to her and wrapped his arms around her. "Let me worry about Blathan. There is a bath, proper clothing and your sister waiting at the river."

"Truly?"

"Truly." He helped her back on the horse, swung up behind her and started them home again. But he could not help himself, he was seething. Dare a man order the death of *his* daughter?

Riding side by side in front of Justin, Shaw and Ginnion exchanged glances. They knew what their laird was thinking and it would be all they could do to keep Justin from going after Keith by himself. They needed a plan and quickly before they got home. Shaw looked back and just as he expected, Justin's eyes were narrowed and his jaw was set.

*

Chisholm was home finally, the courtyard was full of the normal number of barterers and when he looked toward the pasture, he was not surprised to find the MacDuff brothers sleeping with the dog on his back between them. A paw jerked to shoo away a fly, but otherwise none of them stirred. Chisholm smiled, dismounted and let a boy take his horse away. Then he slapped his second on the back, "We found her, she is alive."

The man heaved a great sigh of relief, "Did you truly promise the reward to the MacDuff brothers? They have been pestering me."

"Aye, see that they take their pick."

"Consider it done. I look forward to hearing all about her rescue, but first, you look like death. Have you not slept?"

"Some."

As soon as Chisholm disappeared behind the door of his keep, his second began spreading the word. "MacGreagor's daughter has been found alive." The gossip went from person to person and as soon as the barterers headed home in four different directions, the whole of Scotland would have something new to talk about.

*

Blathan Keith was worried about what to tell his laird, but in the end he only said, "The deed is done." He was grateful not to have to explain further and once Laird Keith nodded, he quickly left the great hall to see his wife and children. The next morning, he was still worried. Eventually word would come either of her death or her rescue, and he hoped for the latter even if he had to pay the price. He had not killed a woman and of that he was glad. Perhaps he could swear he thought she was dead and believed he hit her hard enough to kill her. Perhaps Laird Keith would believe him...he hoped.

*

Just as he promised, her sister and two of Justin's men were waiting for Paisley when they reached the river. They crossed the river first, and then Justin led the way around a bend and found a shallow place in the water where she could bathe without being seen.

Happy to see each other, the sisters embraced and held on for several long moments. The eldest of Justin's daughters, Leslie, wiped her tears of joy away and smiled. "You need a bath."

"Finally someone agrees with me." Paisley headed toward the edge of the water.

"Whose clothing are these?" she asked looking Paisley up and down.

"I have much to tell you." She waited for the men to turn their backs and thought about Macalister's wife. She could not imagine letting them watch and gratefully, none of them dared to. She untied

Rona's dagger, suddenly remembered something and bowed her head.

"What is it, sister?"

"The belt Sawney made for me, I have left it."

Leslie laid the clean clothing and soap down on a rock and put her hands on her hips, "Do not fear, I will protect you from all your brothers."

Paisley couldn't help but smile. "Did you happen to bring another? I care not to put Macalister's belt back on."

"Forgive me, I did not think to, nor did I remember a brush. I was so happy you were safe it was all I could do to remember to bring this much."

Paisley sighed and took off her shoes, "The clan is used to seeing me with wet hair and at least I will not smell." She untied the belt and let the disgusting Macalister plaid fall to the ground. Then she slipped out of her shirt, took the chunk of soap her sister handed her and waded into the water. It was a little bit colder than she expected, but to get clean again she could easily bear it. Careful not to get caught by the river currents, she waded out as far as she could and then submerged to wet her hair.

Sawney's missing belt was just one more insult Macalister managed to put on her and suddenly it was too much. Her tears began again but this time no one could see her.

His back to his nieces, Shaw kept his eyes straight ahead. "What do you mean to do?"

Justin took a deep breath. "I mean to welcome my daughter home and then decide."

It was Justin's way of saying they would discuss it later where

Paisley could not hear and Shaw was satisfied with that. "Perhaps we should have another feast and invite Laird Graham."

"Perhaps we should," Justin agreed.

As soon as she felt clean enough, Paisley walked back out of the water and let her sister gently dry off her sore back while she dried her hair and her front.

Not until Paisley was completely dressed did her sister shout, "You may look now."

*

Adair and Ross MacDuff were having a terrible time deciding which Graham cows they wanted. Just when they chose one, the cow wondered off into the herd. Ross ran this way while Adair ran that and at last, they managed to pin the unruly heifer near a tree. Ross tied one end of the rope around the cow's neck while Adair tied the other end to the tree. Naturally, that wore them both completely out and they were forced to sit down in the pasture to rest.

"That is our only rope," said Adair.

"I know!" a frustrated Ross shot back. "Have we anything to barter for more rope?"

"Only our weapons and who would want them?" Adair looked down at his bent sword and shrugged. "Aleen might take mine, she comments on it often."

"She laughs at it, you mean."

Adair started to argue and then realized his brother was right. "We should have asked for beef *and* rope."

"I think she would have preferred me," Ross muttered, scratching the side of his beard.

"Who?"

"Aleen."

"Aye, but her husband forbids it. Do you see how he glares when we go near her?" asked Adair.

Ross changed hands and scratched the other side of his beard. "Why does he do that, do you suppose?"

"All lads worry their wives will be carried off, witless."

"Witless? If you are so wise, why did you not ask Laird Graham for rope? How are we to get the cows home without more rope?"

Adair wrinkled his brow. "Perhaps we could take one at a time?"

"Perhaps we can at that. 'Twould mean five trips, but we've nothing better to do."

Chisholm was so tired when he got home, he fell asleep the moment he stretched out on his bed. She was safe and nothing else mattered. By the time he awoke and went back outside, the MacDuff brothers were on their horses trying to pull an unwilling cow behind them. He watched them choose the path that would take them home and kept watching until they were out of sight.

There were people still in the marketplace, perhaps more than usual for that time of day and when he went to a table and took an apple, he realized everyone was talking about Paisley's remarkable rescue. Yet more than what happened to her, they wondered to whom Laird MacGreagor would give the golden chalice.

That was one thing Chisholm had not thought about nor did he care. He would much rather have Justin's daughter than his gold. The question now was, how long should he wait to pay his beloved a visit?

Was tomorrow too soon? No, he should give her at least three days to recover. From the way she thanked him only hours before, it was not likely she would choose another man in the next three days. Indeed he would wait and let her rest, although being away from her was already becoming maddening.

*

Never had the clan been so happy as to watch Paisley come home and as soon as they arrived, the uncle Justin left in charge lifted her down and hugged her. Then she was hugged by each or her brothers and her aunts, all of whom were warned about her bruised chin. She patiently answered her youngest brother's endless questions until Sawney took pity and sent him off to play. Instead of going inside, she wanted to walk the stiffness out and Sawney wanted to be with her.

"Can you ever forgive me?" said Sawney, walking arm and arm with her into the glen.

"Can you ever forgive me, I lost your belt?"

"Mine is worse, I lost a sister."

"Did father yell at you?"

"Nay, he was very kind, which made me feel worse. He takes the blame on himself saying he should have sent a lad with you instead of a laddie."

"He called you a laddie? We must think of a way to get even."

Sawney made her stop, hugged her again and then let go. "I am so happy to have you back. I find no joy in trickery without you."

"And I am happy to be back, though I do not suppose I will go to the grave yard again anytime soon."

"I do not blame you." He started them walking again and made certain there were ample guards in the glen this time.

Perplexed, Paisley pointed at a woman. "Who is that?"

"That is laird Monro's daughter, Blanka."

"With Thomas, the same Thomas you hoped I would favor?"

"Aye, they have been together constantly. Thomas is to guard her and I suspect it is not a chore he regrets. He smiles often as does she, but I fear what will happen."

"How so?"

"Her father, Laird Monro, expects Father to marry her."

"So she is the one. Tell me all of it and do not leave out the least detail."

*

Once the greetings were over, Justin went inside the Keep to pour himself a goblet of wine. He was still enraged, but a little calmer now. With just family in the room, he could relax and collect his thoughts.

Moan listened while Ginnion quietly explained Justin's ire. He could certainly see why Justin was upset and he was reluctant to tell his laird more bad news, but it had to be done. Moan waited until Justin sat down and drank half a goblet of wine. He knew he would be expected to report, but he waited a while longer until Ginnion and Shaw also took a seat. "The lad who cut Sawney escaped."

Justin's jaw dropped. "How?"

Moan sat down at the table and shook his head. "He had help...he must have. There is a hole in the back wall and we left nothing inside for him to use to dig it. I saw to that myself."

"Were there no guards?"

"Aye, but they had no cause to watch the back. Who could have guessed we have a…" Moan was hesitant to finish his sentence.

"A traitor?"

"Aye."

Justin closed his eyes and slowly shook his head.

"We cannot be certain it was one of us, "Shaw reminded, "it might have been another Macalister who rescued him."

"Then why did we not find another horse or the lad when we searched for Paisley, and how did he know where we took the one we caught? Nay, we have a traitor and we best find out who it is before more trouble befalls us."

CHAPTER X

Once she was settled in her bed, Justin went into her bedchamber, put a chair next to her and sat down. "Now I will hear all of it."

"Well, I awoke in a bed on the fourth floor of the castle. I knew it was the fourth floor because…"

He listened intently, questioned her in some areas and when she seemed annoyed, he let it go. Having the whole story at last, he kissed her forehead. "Would you like me to stay until you fall asleep?"

"You have nothing better to do?"

Justin smiled. Her former good humor was back and he was glad. He put the chair away just as Blanka came in. "I am happy to know she will not be alone in the night."

"I will see to her."

"She may cry out."

"I will calm her. Sometimes a lass needs another lass to talk to."

"Tell me, are you being well cared for? I'd not like your father to be further upset when I…"

"When you decline his offer?"

Justin had not meant to be so blunt. "Forgive me."

"Laird MacGreagor, I am certain you are a very good lad but I do not want to marry you and I very much hope you will not think unkindly of me. I love another."

"Then we agree." He was so tired, he neglected to ask whom she loved and he did not care, so long as it was not him.

His relief was so evident when he walked out the door, Blanka could not help but giggle. She glanced at Paisley, noticed she was already asleep and quietly began to undress for bed.

*

Morning was unusually quiet in the MacGreagor glen. To awake in her own bed seemed a miracle and the first thing Paisley saw was a new MacGreagor belt draped over the back of her chair. She smiled. She was not as sore as the day before, yet she was not her old self again either. As soon as she dressed, she went down to the great hall.

Abruptly, she stopped on the bottom step. Her four aunts, Blanka and her sister were seated at the table, but there were no men. Paisley walked across the room and found an empty seat next to her sister. "How many did he take?"

"Just three," Ceanna answered.

"Your uncles," said Brenna.

"Save for my husband," Carley added. "He left Moan in command again."

Paisley hung her head. "I tried not to tell him, but…"

Leslie put her hand on her sister's. "We know, dear one, but it is what lads do."

"Particularly our lads," said Patches. "Did we wake you? We sent everyone outside so you could sleep."

"Nay, you did not wake me."

Waiting for Paisley to wake up gave the women a chance to talk and they decided not to ply her with questions. They knew parts of the story, the parts the men told, but not the rest if it. She would tell them everything when she was ready, they all agreed. Yet they were extremely curious and could hardly find anything else to talk about.

"Twill be another fine day," Brenna said.

"A hot one, you mean." Paisley nodded her appreciation to the server who placed a bowl in front of her. She knew her family well and knew they were dying to ask what happened but, she thought, let them wait a little longer. The soft barley porridge and milk went down easy and tasted wonderful. She ate another spoonful and another before she thought of something, quickly swallowed and giggled.

"What?" Nearly all of them asked at once.

"'Tis true Macalister killed his wife, but can you guess why?"

"Nay," Ceanna said while the others shook their heads.

Paisley turned in her chair, scanned the room to be certain there were no men listening before she answered, "She liked for the lads to watch her bathe."

Everyone gasped and then erupted in embarrassed giggles, which soon turned to loud laughter. None of them noticed the server slip out the back door so she could be the first to tell the best gossip she had heard in years.

Their laughter brought Sawney and Moan inside and before long, the room was filled with people all wanting to hear everything there was to hear first hand. Paisley made light of the scary things, mentioned Laird Keith only briefly and heaped mountains of praise on the man who let her go. She left out the part about Chisholm holding her and instead made them laugh with her description of the dog.

Still, she wished she were back in Chisholm's arms. He made her feel safer than anyone else, even her father. She wondered where

Chisholm was and how many days it would be before he came to see her.

Sawney set the golden chalice down in front of her and it was Paisley's turn to gasp. "Never have I seen anything so handsome as this. Where did Father get it?"

Sawney shrugged. "It seems Father has more secrets than we suspected. Shall we search his bedchamber while he is gone?"

His eyes danced with mischief and it made her laugh. "Never have I been brave enough to do that. Think what he would do to us; a month of cleaning up after the horses, in the very least."

Sawney laughed with her but then got serious again. "Sister, there is one thing I do not understand, "How did Laird Macalister know you do not like mutton?"

The room suddenly got quiet. "I cannot even guess. I told him I was already married too, but he dismissed my protests. At the time I thought he meant to make me commit bigamy, but it is odd he knew so much about me."

Sawney glanced at his aunt Carley and then looked down. "We have a traitor."

"What?" Paisley asked.

"We have guards everywhere, how else could the Macalisters get so close to you?" He said no more, but now that he thought about it, the speed with which Neasan got to him after he whistled seemed extraordinary. Neasan's mother and his aunt Carley were close friends and Sawney wanted neither of them hurt, but if the MacGreagors had a traitor, they all needed to know.

Sawney stayed and listened to the conversation until Paisley began to repeat herself. Then he wandered back outside. He took the path that led to the river, found the large flat rock his father preferred and sat down. Normally the rushing river had a calming effect, but not this time. Sawney did not like the feeling of being betrayed and needed to think it through. The question was, what did Neasan hope to gain by Paisley's abduction?

Sawney's eyes suddenly widened. He hoped to start a war with the Kennedys and it did not work. Men sometimes complained about the lack of excitement and war was anything but dull. On the other hand, Justin just left to kill a Keith and perhaps Neasan's intent would be accomplished after all. Suddenly, Sawney could not wait for his father to come home.

*

Chisholm did not come that morning even to inquire about her and Paisley was disappointed. Even if the dog came running to greet her, she would have found some measure of closeness to Chisholm, but alas, there were no visitors at all.

It was odd how much she missed him. The memory of him finding her and holding her tight for such a long time played over and over in her mind. She remembered wanting to touch the side of his face before he went his separate way, as though it was the most natural thing in the world. She had only seen him twice, so how was it possible to have such a yearning for him?

"Paisley?"

"What?" Sawney was standing over her looking down and she suddenly realized she was laying on her back in the glen.

"Are you unwell?"

"Nay, I only wanted to watch the clouds. They drift past so quickly and I hardly ever take the time to watch them. We used to watch them all the time when we were little."

He shook his head to let the guards know not to be concerned, sat down and then stretched out beside her. "I remember. Perhaps we should not have given up childish things as quickly as we did."

"Aye, but we longed to be all grown up." She watched the clouds a while longer before she asked, "Sawney, what do you suppose love is like?"

He lifted his head and nodded, "Like that."

Paisley followed his gaze to Blanka and Thomas who were standing so close together they might as well have been embracing. "It does look like love."

"Father hardly said a word to her last night as we ate. He does not prefer her, does he?"

"He only preferred our mother. What are we to do, then?"

"Do? Why should we do anything?" Sawney asked.

"We must save him from an unhappy marriage and besides, I would like something more to think about than what happened to me."

"Very well then, I say we find the priest, let Thomas and Blanka marry and all will be settled."

"Aye, save what her father will do."

"There is that." Sawney turned on his side to look at her. "Where do you suppose the priest to be this time of year?"

"I never had cause to care where he was, but he cannot be very far away."

"He is at the Graham keep," Thomas said, both he and Blanka

appearing above them.

The mere mention of Chisholm's home, made Paisley smile. "Join us, the grass is soft, the clouds are glorious and I would like your company."

Blanka sank to her knees, turned and soon she was lying down next to Paisley with Thomas doing the same on the other side of her. "They are beautiful. I do not believe I have ever done this."

"Not ever?" asked Paisley.

"Father would never allow such a thing. You do not know how free you are here." She felt Thomas touch her hand with his little finger and didn't move her hand away. Instead, she smiled at him.

"We were just discussing you. My father does not wish to marry and from the looks of the two..." Sawney started. Perhaps he had gone too far.

Thomas turned on his side facing the other three, bent his arm and rested his head on his hand. "Go on, you were about to say from the looks of the two of us, you were thinking what?"

"That we should find the priest and get you married before her father comes back."

When neither of them said anything, Paisley asked, "Is it not what you want?"

"Aye," said Thomas, "but I have not yet asked her."

"Then ask her now," Sawney said. "She might say nay, but I have heard it is a wager all lads must make."

"I would not say nay," Blanka said.

All three of them settled down on their backs again and let the clouds drift by, but this time Thomas had Blanka's whole hand in his.

"Will your father kill my father?" Paisley finally asked.

Blanka rolled her eyes. "If he can. We must keep them apart until Father has calmed."

Paisley hesitated to say anything until her thoughts were fully formed, but she could find no fault in her idea. "We could ride to the Graham keep, you could marry there and neither of our fathers would be the wiser."

"We?" asked Sawney. "This will be a bloody glen if Father finds you were in danger again."

"We can take a guard," said Paisley.

"You are not yet well," Blanka argued.

"I am well enough and I want to go."

"To feast your eyes on Laird Graham?" Sawney teased.

"Nay, to see a dog named, Mutton, and to thank the MacDuff brothers for helping Laird Graham find me. 'Tis the least I can do."

Sawney did not believe a word of it. "And just perhaps feast your eyes on Laird Graham while you are there?"

Paisley giggled, "Perhaps."

"Could we go and come back before Justin returns?" asked Thomas.

Sawney sat up and looked around. Six guards surrounded them, although they were closer to the edge of the forest than to them. "The guards will tell him anyway and I say if we are about to die, we might as well have an adventure first."

Thomas wasn't so sure they should do it, but if it was the only way to have Blanka for his wife he decided he was willing. As soon as he helped her get up, he and his bride-to-be followed Sawney and

Paisley toward the far end of the glen.

Sawney glanced back at the six guards. "They follow us."

"As well they should," said Paisley, then she pointed at a dapple gray. "I believe I prefer that horse?"

"Without a bridle? That, even I will not allow." Sawney took her arm and guided her to the corral. He lifted a bridle off the fence and then whistled and soon, a mare with a brown coat and white markings started toward him. Sawney remembered to reach in a sack hanging on the fence and grab a handful of grain with which to reward the horse. He slipped the bit into its mouth, turned and lifted his sister up.

"You have gotten stronger," said Paisley, knowing that would make her brother proud.

It was only then that the guards began to panic. "Where does she go?" one asked Sawney, a look of horror on his face.

Paisley took the reins Sawney handed to her. "I go for a ride, are you with me?"

"Your father will have my head if I let you go," said the guard.

"I go anyway and he will have your head if you do not protect me."

The guard looked down, "I am a dead lad."

Paisley smiled, "We will wait for you and we will not be gone long, but do not delay." She watched the men race for their horses, smiled when Thomas mounted behind Blanka and her brother did the same behind her. Not long after, the six guards surrounded them and all of them rode out of the glen.

*

The path leading away from MacGreagor land split once, twice and then three times on the way to the village of the Keith. At each crossroads, Justin and his three fully armed brothers-in-law kept right, rode up hills, down again and then across meadows. Fresh horses, the shorter, wider ones better suited for endurance than speed, enabled them to keep from resting often and when the sun was at its highest, the Keith hold came into view.

Undaunted, the four MacGreagors rode the path through the wooden gates into the center of the village, halted and quickly dismounted. They drew their swords and faced all four directions.

"Keith!" Justin shouted. When the door of the Keep did not open, he shouted again. "Keith, I call you out! Arm yourself! "

Laird Keith opened the door slowly and walked out. He was already armed and protected on all sides by his men. "Why do you call me out, MacGreagor?"

"Your lad was seen leaving my daughter's body in a meadow and I have come to kill him. If I must, I will fight you first."

Laird Keith stared at Justin's sword for a moment before he looked into his stern eyes. "He was seen?"

It was an admission. It was the wrong thing to say, and instead of stern eyes, Justin's glare turned to rage. "I will have the lad...now!"

Keith shifted his eyes and then turned to two of his men. "Find Blathan and bring him to me." Instantly, the men took off running up the path to a cottage and before long, they were back, each holding one of Blathan's arms.

"This is the lad?" Justin asked.

"Aye," said Laird Keith, "Do with him as you will."

Justin turned to Shaw and nodded. "See to him."

In turn, Shaw glared at the two men until they released Blathan and backed away, but instead of striking Blathan dead as they expected, Shaw gave Blathan a hearty slap on the back and smiled. "Paisley wants you safe."

"Safe?" Laird Keith stammered. "He is the one who…"

"Aye, and you are the one who ordered it," said Justin.

Keith raised his chin in defiance. "I did no such thing."

"My daughter speaks English."

He was caught, knew he was caught and tried to move behind one of his men. "She is alive?"

"Draw your sword, Keith." Justin demanded. He took a step closer just as Laird Keith tried to hide behind yet another man. Justin put the tip of his sword on the chest of the guard shielding Keith and motioned with his head for him to move aside.

"Protect me, you are to protect me!" Keith whined. Nevertheless, none of Keith's guards were willing to fight a giant and began to inch away.

"Laird MacGreagor, might I be allowed to fight him?"

The voice came from behind Justin and he glanced back to see who it was. When he spotted Blathan, he said, "You want to kill him?"

Blathan walked forward until he stood not far from Justin. "I have wanted to kill him for years. He killed my father without just cause. I will give him the chance he did not give my father, but I *will* kill him."

Justin thought about that for a moment and noticed Blathan was without weapons. "To the lad who spared my daughter, I would grant most anything. Arm yourself and we will see that you are not put upon by his guards." Blathan quickly ran back down the path to his cottage and disappeared inside.

While Blathan was gone, Keith tried to move toward the door of his keep, but Ginnion went to stand in his way. With his legs apart and his arms folded, Ginnion's glare was as fierce as Justin's and he secretly hoped the man would attack him. He would like nothing better than to tear him apart with his bare hands.

Blathan rushed back out the door of his cottage still tying his sword around his waist. Behind him, his wife covered her mouth with her hand and could do nothing but watch. Finally ready, Blathan faced a frightened Keith and pulled his weapon. He put both hands on the handle and prepared to strike.

Striking swords clanked with each opposing strike and men began to shout, some for, but most against Laird Keith. It was a fair fight that lasted for several minutes, with each man suffering only a minor cut at first. Just when it looked like Laird Keith was about to prevail, Blathan got his second wind, swung his sword hard across Keith's chest and made him double over. Then he drove his mighty weapon through Keith's back into his heart.

It was done and Justin was satisfied. He nodded to his men, got on his horse, turned it and started to ride away. Behind him he heard someone ask who the next Laird of the Keiths would be and several shouted, Blathan. Good, Justin thought, he is a fair man whom I shall call friend.

Yet there was one more man he wished to confront before they went home. When they reached the place where the paths crossed, he turned his men toward Macalister's castle.

*

The priest was indeed at the Graham village and no one was more excited than Blanka and Thomas. Nevertheless, it was for Chisholm Paisley looked and when she did not see him, she let her brother help her down off the horse. Instantly she was surrounded by guards and it made her smile. Chisholm would certainly notice a woman surrounded by MacGreagor guards. Just to make certain, she took off her scarf. The clouds were beginning to cool the sweltering heat and although her hair was braided, she was certain to draw attention. Still, where was he?

Paisley watched Thomas talk to the priest near one of the overly laden tables, noticed him giving over the proper donation and then watched him smile at his future bride. This was one wedding she intended to see firsthand and walked that direction. She need not have bothered, the priest urged both Blanka and Thomas to join him in front of the meadow and as soon as the band of MacGreagors arrived, the ceremony began.

Chisholm could not believe his eyes. The crowd outside had quieted for some reason and he went to his second-floor window to see what it was. Then he saw her. He also saw Paisley glance at the others in the growing crowd and he was certain she was looking for him. He had only just finished bathing and was glad of that, but he took a moment to brush his hair and glance in a mirror to be certain his beard and mustache were clean. He hurried down the stairs to join the gathering crowd. He was not surprised that the people seemed more interested in seeing Paisley than witnessing the happy union.

It was not until he made his way closer that he spotted the colors of Blanka's plaid and rolled his eyes. From what Justin told him, Laird

Monro was not going to be pleased, but that was someone else's problem. His problem was to wedge his way between Paisley's guards so he could stand next to her. Finally his mission was accomplished, and when she noticed him, her smile was glowing.

This priest was even more long winded than most and Paisley was glad when it was nearing the end. She did not realize how hard standing still would be after so much walking. At least Chisholm would let her lean against him if she needed and just when she was about to consider doing just that, the wedding was over. Thomas kissed his bride, the crowd cheered and he took his wife for a walk in the meadow where they could be alone.

"You need to sit," Chisholm said.

"Aye, I am not yet well rested."

He dared not touch her in front of her guards, so he stood aside and indicated she should go to his home. Even so, one of the guards rushed on ahead, opened the door and looked inside the empty great hall before he would let Paisley enter.

Paisley was a little chagrined, but she knew they feared what Justin would do if they lost her again and as she expected, they followed her inside. Chisholm's home was pleasant, although it seriously lacked color and even the tall-backed chairs looked uncomfortable. When he pulled a chair away from the table, she was more than happy to sit down even if it was not the best of chairs. He poured a generous portion of water into a goblet, set it down in front of her and took a seat on the opposite side of the table.

"There you are, sister," Sawney said as he came in the door. "Have you seen all the goods on the tables? How is it we have never been here before?"

She smiled. "How is it we have never been anywhere before? Father protects us too well, I have come to think."

Sawney glanced around, "For you, I doubt that will change anytime soon." Then he smiled at Chisholm. "My sister tells me you are the one who found her. I thank you for that, since I am the one who lost her."

Paisley looked at Chisholm too, "I do not believe my brother will ever forgive himself."

"I quite understand," said Chisholm.

Sawney again looked at the blank walls. "Do you find it difficult to hang a tapestry or two? 'Twould do the place no harm."

Paisley was horrified. "Swayne, you are being unkind. Perhaps Laird Graham does not have the means…"

"I have tapestries aplenty," Chisholm interrupted. "They are stored until the time is right."

"When will that be?" Sawney wanted to know.

"When I have taken a wife. A wife who does the choosing, I have heard, is a much happier wife." Chisholm thoughtfully stroked his beard for a moment. "Would you care to see them?"

Paisley's eyes lit up. "I would like it very much. Our tapestries are getting old and perhaps Father will barter for one or two, that is if your wife does not prefer them."

He smiled, "If I am fortunate enough to have the right wife, perhaps your father will have more tapestries than even he can hang."

His meaning was not lost on her and she blushed. This was the happiness she dreamed of and it seemed to be coming true sooner than she expected. When he stood, she stood as well, and after the guards made certain it was safe, she followed him out the door. She noticed Sawney was beside her and she would rather he were not. "You need not attend me so closely."

"I do not *need* it either, but I will have a look at these tapestries too."

There seemed no way to be shed of him, so she decided ignoring him was best. As soon as Chisholm opened the door to his personal store house, the guards once more went in to be certain it was safe. At last, she was let in and there was no mistaking the pride in Chisholm's smile.

"Some are old and not so very good," he began, "but others..." he made his way between stacked trunks to the back, lifted a rolled up tapestry and began to spread it out on top of the trunks for her to see.

It was a magnificent portrait of a Graham mother and her child against a light blue background. It was made of fine woolen threads that felt extraordinarily soft when Paisley ran her fingers over it. She looked up just in time to see how pleased he was with it. "'Tis glorious."

"And this is but one. At last count, there were fifteen very good ones to choose from," said Chisholm.

"What is in the trunks," asked Sawney.

"Nothing of much value, but you are welcome to look. They are weapons no longer in use mostly." He shoved the tapestry aside and opened the lid to the top trunk. When he did, particles of dust filled the air and it was obvious he had not opened that trunk in a while. "There are some very fine wood carvings in this one."

Sawney was excited to see each new piece and lifted one to show his sister, only to find the next equally as wonderful.

The dust was getting to Paisley, so she moved back a little. Soon the man she loved was standing beside her and feeling his nearness was about to completely consume her. She wanted him to hold her again and make her feel safe the way he had before.

Chisholm was struggling to contain his desires too. It was time to say something more, so he leaned down and whispered, "If you wish it so, you will be mistress of all this."

She slowly turned and stared at him. Is that what he thought she wanted -- to be mistress over his belongings? She had forgotten to breathe until now and suddenly felt the need to fill her lungs. Only she feared she would soon explode, calmed herself and whispered back. "Tis not good enough."

Chisholm was completely taken aback and he did not bother to keep his voice low. "What is not good enough? Is it my home, do you desire a bigger keep? I am aware yours is…"

Paisley rolled her eyes. "I came to thank you and thank you I have. Sawney, we are leaving."

Her brother was almost as shocked as Chisholm and when he turned, he let the trunk lid fall making an even larger puff of dust. By the time he looked, Paisley was already out the door with Chisholm right behind her. He would have liked staying longer, but something upset her and Sawney was well aware that when his sister had her mind set, there was no changing it. All he could do was hurry to catch up with her.

"What is not good enough?" Chisholm watched her guards escort her back to the horses and tried again. "Tell me and I will make it better?" he shouted.

She stopped and turned back to face him. "We are to have a feast in three days. Bring the MacDuff brothers… if you can tear yourself away from…" She threw her hands up in defeat, "all this splendor."

Sawney lifted her up on the horse, mounted, waited for the guards to surround them and started to leave. Suddenly he halted his horse. "We have forgotten Blanka and Thomas." He whistled, waited and before long, Thomas and Blanka came out of the trees and ran for their horse.

At all this, a very confused Chisholm could only stare until the MacGreagors rode out of sight. "Splendor?" he mumbled. "First it is not good enough and then she calls it splendor?"

CHAPTER XI

Paisley could not believe it. He seemed to love her, but how dare he think he needed to tempt her with wealth? She wanted to scream or throw something. Unfortunately, her guards would get upset if she did. They were probably eager to get home before her father did and she could not blame them for that. Blanka and Thomas were now married and that was the purpose of their visit.

Chisholm was not nearly as handsome as she thought he was at the feast. She could never marry a man who thought only of his wealth and not of love. In her anger, she invited him to their next feast, a welcome home just for her, and now she regretted it. She would be pleasant, she decided, but her smiles would not be for him. Instead, she would stay as far away from him as she could.

"What about the dog?" Sawney asked. He had his arm around his sister's waist, could feel her tension and decided he should try to calm her.

"What dog?"

Sawney smiled, "Did we not come to see a dog and the MacDuff brothers? I would have liked staying long enough to see the dog."

Paisley playfully smacked his arm, "Believe me when I say, if the dog were there, you would have seen him."

"Do you want to tell me what has upset you?"

She closed her eyes and leaned back against him. "Nay, it will pass soon enough. Besides, we've enough to fret over. What are we to do when Laird Monro returns?"

*

All the way from the Keith's, Justin thought about how to get the Macalisters to give up the man who hurt Paisley. With Macalister dead, they might not have chosen a new laird yet and therefore, there would be no one with whom he could negotiate. He would rather just go home and let the nightmare be over with, but he had a reputation to uphold for the sake of his children and his clan. There was a price to pay for any man who hurt a MacGreagor, the time to have it over with was now, and he boldly rode up the path to do just that.

The last person Rona wanted to see was Justin MacGreagor. This time, he came with only three warriors into the Macalister courtyard, but she feared him just as much. She thought first about where to hide her nephew, decided the boy would probably not be harmed and then feared for her brother.

"Bring me the lad who hurt my daughter!" Justin bellowed.

Inside the castle, Rona trembled. Yet Justin had believed a lie before, perhaps he would again. She hurried down the last flight of stairs, pulled open both of the large wooden doors and stepped out. She was too late. Laird MacGreagor had already dismounted, drawn his sword and her brother was standing in front of him. Rona caught her breath.

Justin glared at the man and then noticed he held a baby in each arm. His determination quickly turned to ire. "You dare hide behind wee ones?"

"Nay," said the man. "I dare hurt your daughter to keep Macalister from killing mine." His words hung in the air for a long moment before the man saw Justin lower his eyes. "I would do it again," he muttered.

Justin took a deep breath. "I would do the same." Yet he did not put his sword away and instead began to look the people over. "What of the other lad?"

"Gone," Rona's brother answered. "He returned in the night, took his belongings and rode away."

"I have a traitor in my clan; do you know who it is?"

"Nay, I only did as I was told and saw no others."

Justin believed him and at length put his sword away and got back on his horse. He nodded to Shaw and then suddenly realized he had ignored the woman who saved Paisley. Once more he got down off his horse and walked to her. "My daughter is well and sends her regards. She wishes me to thank you."

Rona's nerves were still a bit on edge, but she managed to curtsy and when Justin walked away, both knew the nightmare Macalister created was finally over. Pleased, Rona turned around and looked at the new wall decorations in the great hall. Already the place was looking better and letting in the fresh air did wonders to rid it of the smell of mold. Tomorrow or the next day, she intended to visit the soothsayers to see if they had a remedy for such a thing as mold.

She might not always live there, especially after the clan chose a new laird, but while she did, she intended to make it a happy place for herself, the old man and her nephew.

*

Blanka went back inside the MacGreagor great hall and up the stairs to bed just before Justin and the men rode their horses into the courtyard. She was a married woman, but spending the night with her husband would have to wait until they had time to explain things.

Downstairs, the great hall was still full of people. Justin's sisters greeted their husbands while Paisley hugged her father. "Blathan?" she asked.

"Safe. He killed Keith and I believe he will be the new laird."

"Good." Paisley turned and stared up the stairs.

"Wait, have you nothing to tell your father?" Moan went to the bottom of the stairs and looked up at her.

Slowly, Paisley came back down. "What?"

"You know what," said Moan.

Justin frowned, "I cannot wait, what have you done, daughter?"

She lowered her eyes. "Nothing so awful as all that. I merely went for a ride."

"To see Laird Graham," Sawney put in. "I went with her as did her guards and she was safe, father."

Justin turned to Moan, "You let her go?"

"Let her, how was I to stop her?"

"Father, you did not say I could *not* go riding," Paisley reminded.

Justin looked at Ginnion and then at Shaw, both of whom still had their arms around their wives. "I do not recall, did I?"

"I recall," said Shaw. "You did *not* forbid it."

"Aye, but who could guess she would want to?" He turned his attention back to Paisley. "Did you see Laird Graham?"

Paisley let the disgust show in her expression. "I wish never to hear that name again!" With that, she hurried up the stairs to bed.

*

At the noon meal the next day, everyone was excited to talk about the coming feast and the decision -- who deserved the golden chalice?

"Paisley, you decide," Justin said, filling his spoon with tasty morsels of beef and cabbage.

"I cannot. Rona helped me get away, Blathan refused to kill me and…"

When she paused, Sawney added, "Laird Graham found you. Why do you think he searched for you?"

Paisley glared at her brother while everyone else laughed. "I said not to say that name!"

"Aye, but…" Just then, the whistles sounded and Sawney jumped up to run up the stairs. He hoped it was Laird Graham, but from his sister's window, he saw the army of men and knew exactly who it was. "Monro!" With much less excitement, he walked back down the stairs. "Tis your father, Blanka."

Blanka tried not to react, but this was the moment she feared most. She looked pleadingly at Sawney and as if he understood, watched him walk out the door. Hopefully, Sawney would bring Thomas back.

Next she looked at Justin and he appeared just as tormented as she felt. She stood up and began to ring her hands. "What will you tell him?"

Justin stood up too, as did the other men and prepared himself to meet her father. "I will say I have no want of a wife." He watched her reaction and discovered she was not as pleased as he expected. What was she so upset about?

In his usual flare, Laird Monro burst into the room, neglected the pleasantries and walked straight to Justin. This time both Shaw and Ginnion moved closer to protect their laird.

"Well," roared Monro, "have you bed her yet?"

Justin nodded for his eldest sister to take the other women and children out and waited until they were gone.

"I did not, nor will I marry her!"

"You know very well you may *not* refuse to marry her, MacGreagor. She has been under your roof and 'tis not proper for an unmarried lad and an unmarried lass to share the same roof."

"It was you who put her under my roof, not me." Justin quickly glanced at Blanka and noticed she had moved even further away. "What is her crime? Why do you try so hard to be shed of her?

Monro was not used to having anyone stand up to him, let alone ask such personal questions and this particular question took him by surprise. Even more surprising were his daughter's words.

"Aye, father what is my crime?"

Monro gritted his teeth, "I do not answer to you!"

"Then you will answer to me," Thomas said coming in the door with Sawney right behind him.

Monro slowly turned around to see who dared talk to him that way. "Who are you?"

"I am your daughter's husband."

Blanka caught her breath, Justin's jaw dropped and Shaw and Ginnion rushed forward to keep Monro from striking Thomas. Thomas was a much stronger man, would not take kindly to it and Monro had left his guard outside.

Again Monro gritted his teeth, "Say a prayer lad, you are about to die."

Blanka ran to him and grabbed her father's arm. "You would kill the lad I love?"

"Blanka, you are the daughter of a laird and I wished you to marry a laird."

Blanka returned his glare and put her hands on her hips. "What is done is done and even you cannot change it. I will live here with my husband and that is an end to it!"

Justin noticed when Sawney came to stand beside him. "Is it true?" he whispered.

"Aye, the priest was at the Graham hold."

"Remind me to thank you later."

At last Monro relented and accepted his daughter's fate. He stayed for all of an hour more before he finally hugged his Blanka and wished her well. Then he mounted his horse and led his army away.

It was over and both were happy when Thomas walked his wife to one of the older cottages, which had just become her new home.

*

It was two nights of badly needed glorious sleep for the MacGreagor clan before the day of the feast arrived. This time, a wild boar cooked in the pit and filled the air with the mouth-watering aroma of ham. The women again tended the cooking while the men hauled out the tables and set up the games.

In the late morning, Chisholm Graham rode up the glen with his guard and the MacDuff brothers. They were the clans only invited guests and with no others to wait for, soon the games would begin.

Paisley watched from her window until they were half way there and then spotted the dog. "Uh oh." She grabbed a sack and made it down the stairs and out the door, before the deerhound decided he'd had enough of his good behavior and began to race toward all those new faces he aimed to lick.

"Mutton!" She called his name just in time to keep him from mowing down two little girls. With leaps and bounds, Mutton reached her in the blink of an eye, jumped up and let her rub the back of his ears.

"I have saved a bone for you, but you must sit." The dog obeyed, but not so happily so, glancing at a man he hoped to greet and then at a woman before Paisley managed to pull a large bone out of the sack. With sheer delight in his eyes, he grabbed the bone, raced back into the glen and laid down. Paisley smiled, but when she saw Chisholm coming closer, she set the sack down against the wall, turned away, walked through the crowd and went to talk to her brother. She could hardly avoid the man for hours, but she was determined to try.

Chisholm noticed her reaction to him and guessed she had not forgiven him for whatever it was he did wrong. After hours of replaying it in his mind, he still did not understand. At one point, he decided if she was so quick to anger, perhaps she was the wrong woman for him after all. Then he remembered what it was like to hold her in his arms. Now he was where he wanted to be - in the same glen, the same village and the same courtyard she was in.

A boy took his horse away after Chisholm dismounted, his men drifted off to talk to the MacGreagor men and the MacDuff brothers shyly got off their horses and stood outside the courtyard taking it all in. Chisholm ignored Paisley and went into the Keep to greet Justin.

Adair watched to his left while Ross MacDuff watched to his right. The only time they had been in the glen was once when they snuck in late at night. Suddenly Paisley was standing before them smiling and it was the first time they had seen of her up close.

"I have changed my mind," Adair whispered, staring at her uncovered hair and her sparkling blue eyes. "I will have her for my wife."

"As will I," Ross mumbled.

Paisley had never met a man the same height as she and it made her want to giggle. Still she composed herself and curtsied. "I have heard you helped Laird Graham find me and I wish to thank you for it." She couldn't help but notice both brothers blush. "You are welcome here and may come anytime. You are also welcome to all you can eat and if I am not mistaken, the meal is almost ready. Do you like ham?"

*

Inside the Keep, Chisholm accepted the goblet of wine Justin handed him and downed half. He needed it, he thought, now that he feared Paisley was no longer his.

The only two still inside the Keep, Justin asked, "What have you done?"

The question surprised Chisholm and he wrinkled his brow. "In what regard?"

"My daughter refuses to let us speak your name. Have you offended her?"

"Apparently so." He rubbed the back of his neck for a moment. "I do not know what I said."

Justin sat down in his usual place at the head of the table and nursed his drink. "When you take a wife, you will soon learn what a lad says is not always what a lass hears."

"You must be right. One moment she was admiring my tapestries and the next she was gone."

"Do you still love my daughter?"

"Very much," Chisholm admitted.

"Did you manage to tell her so?"

"I wanted to, but her guards and Sawney would not allow the possibility."

Justin playfully slapped Chisholm on the back. "Should she let you near her again, which I doubt, you might try saying that first."

Chisholm nodded and then downed the rest of his drink. "If she lets me near her again."

Outside, Justin was enjoying himself to the fullest. Wherever Chisholm was, Paisley managed to be somewhere else. The games began and Chisholm cheered when a Graham won the log contest, but Paisley decided to watch the archers instead. Chisholm moved to the archers just as Paisley drifted off to see about the horseshoe toss, and it was at that point Chisholm gave up.

Justin was about to lose his daughter again, but to the man who found her and if he loved her that much, Chisholm deserved Paisley. All fathers had to let go of their daughters and the Graham village was not that far away, he reasoned. According to Leslie, he was about to welcome his first grandchild too, which made him both proud and feeling his age.

*

It was nearly time to eat and the MacDuff brothers, as well as their dog, went to watch the men lift the meat of the wild boar out of the pit in the ground. The warriors cut the meat and placed large chunks of it on wooden platters to be carried to the table. Mutton could not help himself and although he sat as he was told, he licked his lips repeatedly.

Taking pity on the dog, one of the men gave him a hock bone, meat and all, and there was no happier dog in Scotland. At last it was time for the people to eat, and about this, the MacDuff brothers were not bashful. They tasted it all, decided what they liked and went back for more.

Chisholm sat beside Justin, ate his fill and watched Paisley ignore him. He was wondering if he would have to go home without even a smile from her when Justin stood up and called for the crowd to quiet.

Justin cleared his throat and began, "It was not an easy decision for there were many who helped recover Paisley. I have decided Chisholm Graham deserves the golden chalice." Justin picked it up off the table, and handed it to Chisholm.

Laird Graham stood up, admired it for a moment and when he looked, Paisley was actually watching him. "I am greatly pleased, but I would not have found her without the help of the MacDuff brothers and their dog. I have no need of wealth; therefore I give it over to the two lads who deserve it." He walked to Adair, handed the chalice to him and then walked back to stand beside Justin.

It was as though the brothers were alone in the glen for they ignored the cheers of the crowd completely. "Five beef and a golden chalice? With so much wealth we can start our own clan," said Adair.

Ross took it out of his brother's hands, looked it over and then started down the glen for their swaybacked horses. "Without wives?"

"We will have wives once I am laird."

"You? I am the strong one and a laird must be strong."

Adair rolled his eyes. "Aye, but I am the handsome one and a laird must be…"

Their voices faded, the people laughed and the dog scrambled to catch up. Mutton abruptly stopped, briefly looked back and once more decided to go with the brothers.

Chisholm was so distracted by the MacDuffs, he did not notice when Paisley walked to him. "You do not want the chalice?"

He was afraid of saying the wrong thing again and merely said, "Nay."

"Then what reward do you require?"

"Come with me and I will tell you." He reached for her hand and when she did not pull away, he led the way around the corner of the Keep and down the path toward the river. Then he let go and just walked beside her. "I want children, a wife that loves me and most of all, I want to marry the lass *I* love."

She took a few more steps toward the river before she asked, "Who do you love?"

"Do you not know?"

Paisley puffed her cheeks, "'Tis still not good enough."

She started to walk back the way they came and he grabbed her hand just in time. "I love you. I have loved you for quite a long time, though I did not realize it until lately."

At last, she turned to look at him. "I have loved you less than a fortnight. Is it enough to make a happy marriage?"

"It is for me, but if you tell me to wait until you are certain, I will."

For days she wanted to put her hand on the side of his face and now she could. "I long for you when you are not with me. Is that love?"

"It must be, I long for you too." He let go of her hand, put his arms around her and pulled her to him. Then he watched her lift her face and close her eyes. At first, he only brushed his lips against hers. Then he felt her begin to lean heavily against him, knew she was ready and kissed her with as much passion as he dared.

Watching from up the path, Sawney rushed back to his father. "He is kissing her."

Justin grinned. "Perhaps we should find the priest."

*

The wedding the following week was a grand affair with all the MacGreagors watching as well as several of the Graham men and their wives. Chisholm stood next to his first and second in command, while Paisley was attended by members of her vast family. Once the ceremony was ended and a kiss sealed their commitment, Paisley went inside the Keep, up the stairs and to her bedchamber with her sister.

She was so excited, she had trouble standing still enough to let Leslie help her change from the colors of her father into the colors of her husband. Then she went back and enjoyed the merriment until it was time. Sitting her horse beside a happy Chisholm's, she waved one last time to her family and then rode off to become mistress of the

Grahams.

*

There was but one thing still on Justin's mind and after the young couple rode away and most everyone else went to bed, he put his arm around Carley. "I wish to have a word with you."

Carley was next to the youngest of Justin's sisters and knew what was coming. The clan had a traitor and there was no doubt in her mind who it was -- it was the son of her best friend.

Justin took a candle off the table in the great hall, led Carley up the two flights of stairs where no one could hear and opened the door to his bedchamber.

Just then, Sawney stuck his head out of the second-floor bedchamber he shared with Hew, "May I have Paisley's room, father?"

Justin looked down the stairs at his son and thought of something. "Come with me." He waited for his son to enter, closed the door behind him and waited until both sat down at the table before he seated himself. Then he took Carley's hands in his, "You know what I must do."

"Must you?"

"Sister, there is little doubt. Neasan is our traitor and I must not let him live."

"Brother, his mother is unwell and the death of her son will surely kill her too. Is there no other way?"

"I could banish him, but as my father said, a banished man waits behind every tree to seek his revenge."

A tear began to roll down Carley's cheek. "There must be

something other to do."

"Sister, if I let him live, I will only have to fight him on another day. I could never trust him, nor rely on him to safely guard us."

"He knows you suspect him, father."

"I know and I am surprised he does not run off," said Justin.

Carley wiped a tear off her cheek. Whatever else he is, he does not leave his mother to face the shame of his running off. She believes it was not him and truly, we have no witness."

"True," Sawney agreed.

Justin got up and began to pace. For a long time, Carley and Sawney just let him think and when Carley looked as though she needed comfort Sawney took her hand.

"Perhaps there is another way," said Justin finally. "I will send him, and two others I find unpleasant, off to find something for me."

"What?" asked Carley.

"A sea monster."

"Father, we have heard they are very large. They can hardly bring back a sea monster."

"Aye, but they can bring back a bone that will tell us just how large they are."

Carley heaved a sigh of relief. "I would like the sight of such a thing myself."

Justin retook his seat. "When they return, I will think of something else and if I am no longer with you, Sawney will know what to do."

"Perhaps I might like a Viking spear from the far north," Sawney said.

Justin smiled. "I believe you deserve a bedchamber of your own."

*

In the great hall of the Graham hold two days later, Chisholm finished pounding a small wooden peg into the wall at the corner of Paisley's favorite tapestry. Then he moved back to stand beside his wife and admire it. She chose one with a dark blue background that depicted a long haired Scottish cow and twin calves.

Suddenly, there were shouts outside and Chisholm rushed out the door to see what it was with Paisley right behind him. A crowd had already gathered near the meadow and from behind it, Paisley was too short to see, so he took her hand, led her back inside and up the stairs to the window in their second-floor bedchamber.

In the meadow, the MacDuff brothers were trying to catch their fifth cow. Chisholm put his arms around her from behind and said, "I promised them four cows and one bull. Yet they chase another cow. Do you suppose they do not know the difference?"

Paisley giggled. Rain the day before caused the brothers to slide in the mud, but they were determined. First Ross grabbed one around the neck and held on, but the cow was not deterred and kept right on walking. Adair, pleased with his brother's accomplishment slipped once, then twice, in the mud trying to catch up so he could tie the rope around her neck.

Just as he was about to succeed, the cow jerked her head, tossed Ross off, and when he landed on his backside the crowd roared with laughter. First a drop of rain fell, then another and soon the heavy downpour made the people run for cover, but the brothers did not care. They finally managed to separate their target from the herd and were last seen running after it down a hill and up the other side.

Paisley turned in her husband's arms. "I do love you so."

He smiled and tightened his hold on her, "I am happy to hear that. Promise you will say it often."

"I promise." Once more, she looked up into his eyes, grinned and got lost in his passion.

~The end~

Coming Soon – Book 3 in the Viking series.

MORE MARTI TALBOTT BOOKS

Marti Talbott's Highlander Series: books 1 – 5 are short stories that follow the MacGreagor clan through two generations. They are followed by:

Betrothed, Book 6

The Golden Sword, Book 7

Abducted, Book 8

A Time of Madness, Book 9

Triplets, Book 10

Secrets, Book 11

Choices, Book 12

Ill-Fated Love Book 13

The Other Side of the River, Book 14

The Viking Series:

The Viking, Book 1 explains how the clan came into being.

The Viking's Daughter, Book 2

Book 3 is coming soon.

Marblestone Mansion (Scandalous Duchess Series) follows the MacGreagor clan into Colorado's early 20th century. There are currently 10 books in this series.

The Jackie Harlan Mysteries

Seattle Quake 9.2, Book 1

Missing Heiress, Book 2

Greed and a Mistress, Book 3

The Carson Series

The Promise, Book 1

Broken Pledge, Book 2

Talk to Marti on Facebook at:

https://www.facebook.com/marti.talbott

Sign up to be notified when new books are published at:

http://www.martitalbott.com

CPSIA information can be obtained at www.ICGtesting.com
Printed in the USA
BVOW05s1842080615

403701BV00002B/117/P